About th

Anthony Horowitz was brought up on horror stories, and his childhood love of all things sinister and scary has stayed with him. The stories in this book are inspired by ordinary, everyday objects and events, as are most of the stories in the rest of the series. But each of them has a twist to remind us that even in a safe, predictable world, the horrible and unexpected, the blood-curdling and the spine-chilling, are never far away.

Anthony Horowitz is the highly successful author of a bestselling range of books, including detective stories, adventure stories and spy stories which have been translated into over a dozen languages. He is also a well-known television screenwriter with credits including *Poirot, Midsomer Murders* and *Foyle's War*. Anthony lives in East London.

'A first class children's novelist'
TIMES EDUCATIONAL SUPPLEMENT

'Perfect for readers with an appetite for ghoulish happenings'
SCHOOL LIBRARIAN ASSOCIATION

'Suspenseful and exciting'
BOOKS FOR KEEPS

ANTHONY
HOROWITZ
HORROR
2

WHATEVER YOU DO, DON'T TURN OUT THE LIGHT...

ORCHARD BOOKS

Orchard Books
338 Euston Road, London NW1 3BH
Orchard Books Australia
Hachette Children's Books
Level 17/207 Kent Street, Sydney, NSW 2000

First published by Orchard Books in 2000
This edition published in 2008
Text copyright © Anthony Horowitz 1999

The right of Anthony Horowitz to be identified
as the author of this work has been asserted by him
in accordance with the Copyright, Designs and Patents Act, 1988.

A CIP catalogue record for this book is available from the British Library

ISBN 978 1 84616 970 0

1 3 5 7 9 10 8 6 4 2

www.orchardbooks.co.uk

Printed and bound in Great Britain by CPI Bookmarque, CR0 4TD

Orchard Books is a division of Hachette Children's Books,
an Hachette Livre UK company.
www.hachettelivre.co.uk

CONTENTS

THE HITCHHIKER

Why did my father have to stop? I told him not to. I knew it was a bad idea. Of course, he didn't listen to me. Parents never do. But it would never have happened if only he'd driven on.

We'd been out for the day, just the three of us, and what a great, really happy day it had been. My fifteenth birthday, and they had taken me to Southwold, a small town on the Suffolk coast. We'd got there just in time for lunch and had spent the afternoon walking on the beach, looking in the shops and losing money in the crummy arcade down by the pier.

A lot of people would think that Southwold was a rubbish place to go, especially on your birthday. But they'd be wrong. The truth is that it's special. From the multicoloured beach huts that have probably been there since Queen Victoria's time, to the cannons on the cliff which have certainly been there a whole lot longer. It's got a lighthouse and a brewery and a sloping village green that all look as if they've come out of an Enid Blyton story. None of the shops seem to sell anything that anyone would actually want and there's one, in the High Street, that has these fantastic wooden toys. A whole circus that comes to life for twenty pence. And the talking head of Horatio Nelson who puts his telescope up to his missing eye and sings. You get real fish and chips in Southwold. Fish that were still swimming while you were driving to the restaurant. Sticky puddings with custard. I don't need to go on. The whole place is so old-fashioned and so English that it just makes you want to smile.

We started back at about five o'clock. There was a real Suffolk sunset that evening. The sky was pink and grey and dark blue and somehow there was almost too much of it. I sat in the back of the car and as the door slammed I felt that strange, heavy feeling you get at the end of a really good day. I was sad that it was over. But I felt happy and tired, glad that it was over too.

It was only about an hour's drive and as we left Southwold it began to rain. There's nothing strange about that. The weather often changes rapidly in Suffolk. By the time we reached the A12, the rain was falling quite heavily, slanting down, grey needles in the breeze. And there, ahead of us on the road, was a man, walking quickly, his hands clenched on the sides of his jacket, pulling it around him. He didn't turn round as we approached but he must have heard us coming. Suddenly his hand shot out. One thumb jutted out; the universal symbol of the hitchhiker. He wanted a lift.

There were about fifteen seconds until we reached him. My father was the first to speak.

'I wonder where he's going.'

'You're not going to stop,' my mother said.

'Why not? It's a horrible evening. Look at the weather!'

And there you have my parents. My father is a dentist and maybe that's why he's always trying to be nice to people. He knows that nobody in their right mind really wants to see him. He's tall and shambolic, the sort of man who goes to work with his hair unbrushed and with socks that don't match. My mother works three days a week at an estate agency. She's much tougher than him. When I was young, she was always the one who would send me to bed. He'd let me stay up all night if she wasn't there.

There's one more thing I have to tell you about them. They both look quite a bit older than they actually are. There's a reason for this. My older brother, Eddy. He died suddenly when he was twelve years old. That was nine years ago and my parents have never really recovered. I miss him too. Of course, he bullied me sometimes like all big brothers do, but his death was a terrible thing. It hurt us all and we know that the pain will never go away.

Anyway, it was typical of my dad to want to stop and offer the man a lift and just as typical of my mum to want to drive on. In the back seat, I said, 'Don't stop, Dad.' But it was already too late. Just fifteen seconds had passed since we saw the hitchhiker and already we were slowing down. I'd told him not to stop. But I'd no sooner said it than we did.

The rain was coming down harder now and it was very dark so I couldn't see very much of the man. He seemed quite large, towering over the car. He had long hair, hanging down over his eyes.

My father pressed the button that lowered the window. 'Where are you going?' he asked.

'Ipswich.'

Ipswich was about twenty miles away. My mother didn't say anything. I could tell she was uncomfortable.

'You were heading there on foot?' my father asked.

'My car's broken down.'

'Well – we're heading that way. We can give you a lift.'

'John…' My mother spoke my father's name quietly but already it was too late. The damage was done.

'Thanks,' the man said. He opened the back door.

I suppose I'd better explain.

The A12 is a long, dark, anonymous road that often

goes through empty countryside with no buildings in sight. It was like that where we were now. There were no street lights. Pulled in on the hard shoulder, we must have been practically invisible to the other traffic rushing past. It was the one place in the world where you'd have to be crazy to pick up a stranger.

Because, you see, everyone knows about Fairfields. It's a big, ugly building not far from Woodbridge, surrounded by a wall that's fifteen metres high with spikes along the top and metal gates that open electrically. The name is quite new. It used to be called the East Suffolk Maximum Security Prison for the Criminally Insane. And right now we were only about ten miles away from it.

That's the point I'm trying to make. When you're ten miles away from a lunatic asylum, you don't stop in the dark to pick up someone you've never met. You have to say to yourself that maybe, just maybe, there could have been a break-out that night. Maybe one of the loonies has cut the throat of the guard at the gate and slipped out into the night. And so it doesn't matter if it's raining. It doesn't even matter if the local nuclear power station at Sizewell has just blown up and it's coming down radioactive slush. You just don't stop.

The back door slammed shut. The man eased himself into the back seat, rain water glistening on his jacket. The car drove forward again.

I looked at him, trying to make out his features in the half light. He had a long face with a square chin and small, narrow eyes. His skin was pale, as if he hadn't been outdoors in a while. His hair was somewhere between brown and grey, hanging down in clumps. His clothes looked old and second-hand. A sports jacket and baggy corduroys. The sort of clothes a gardener might wear. His fingers were unusually long. One hand was resting on his thigh and his fingers reached all the way to his knee.

'Have you been out for the day?' he asked.

'Yes.' My father knew he had annoyed my mother and he was determined to be cheerful and chatty, to show that he wasn't ashamed of what he'd done. 'We've been in Southwold. It's a beautiful place.'

'Oh yes.' He glanced at me and I saw that he had a scar running over his eye. It began on his forehead and ended on his cheek and it seemed to have pushed the eye a little to one side. It wasn't quite level with the other one.

'Do you know Southwold?' my father asked.

'No.'

'So where have you come from today?'

The man thought for a moment. 'I broke down near Lowestoft,' he said and somehow I knew he was lying. For a start, Lowestoft was a long way away, right on the border with Norfolk. If he'd broken down there, how could he have managed to get all the way to Southwold? And why bother? It would have been easier to jump on a train and go straight to Ipswich. I opened my mouth to say something but the man looked at me again, more sharply this time. Maybe I was imagining it but he could have been warning me. Don't say anything. Don't ask any difficult questions.

'What's your name?' my mother asked. I don't know why she wanted to know.

'Rellik,' he said. 'Ian Rellik.' He smiled slowly. 'This your son in the back?'

'Yes. That's Jacob. He's fifteen today.'

'His birthday?' The man uncurled his hand and held it out to me. 'Happy birthday, Jacob.'

'Thank you.' I took the hand. It was like holding a dead fish. At the same time I glanced down and saw that his sleeve had pulled back exposing his wrist. There was something glistening on his skin and it wasn't rain water. It was dark red, trickling down all the way to the edge of his hand, rising over the fleshy part of his thumb.

Blood!

Whose blood? His own?

He pulled his hand away, hiding it behind him. He knew I had seen it. Maybe he wanted me to.

We drove on. A cloud must have burst because it was really lashing down. You could hear the rain thumping on the car roof and the windscreen wipers were having to work hard to sweep it aside. I couldn't believe we'd been walking on the beach only a few hours before.

'Lucky we got in,' my mother said, reading my mind.

'It's bad,' my father said.

'It's hell,' the man muttered. Hell. It was a strange choice of word. He shifted in his seat. 'What do you do?' he asked.

'I'm a dentist.'

'Really? I haven't seen a dentist…not for a long time.' He ran his tongue over his teeth. The tongue was pink and wet. The teeth were yellow and uneven. I guessed he hadn't cleaned them in a while.

'You should go twice a year,' my father said.

'You're right. I should.'

There was a rumble of thunder and at that exact moment the man turned to me and mouthed two words. He didn't say them. He just mouthed them, making sure my parents couldn't see.

'You're dead.'

I stared at him, completely shaken. At first I thought I must have misunderstood him. Maybe he had said something else and the words had got lost in the thunderclap. But then he nodded slowly, telling me that I wasn't wrong. That's what he'd said. And that's what he meant.

I felt every bone in my body turn to jelly. That thing about the asylum. When we'd stopped and picked up the hitchhiker, I hadn't *really* believed that he was a madman who'd just escaped. Often you get scared by things but you can still tell yourself that it's just your imagination, that you're being stupid. And after all, there are lots of stories about escaped lunatics and none of them are ever true. But now I wasn't so sure. Had I imagined it? Had he said something else? *You're dead.* I thought back, picturing the movement of his lips. He'd said it all right.

We were doing about forty miles per hour, punching through the rain. I turned away, trying to ignore the man on the seat beside me. Mr Rellik. There was something strange about that name and without really thinking I found myself writing it on the window, using the tip of my finger.

R E L L I K

The letters, formed out of the condensation inside the car, hung there for a moment. Then the two 'l's in the middle began to run. It reminded me of blood. The name sounded Hungarian or something. It made me think of someone in *Dracula*.

'Where do you want us to drop you?' my mother asked.

'Anywhere,' Mr Rellik said.

'Where do you live in Ipswich?'

There was a pause. 'Blade Street,' he said.

'Blade Street? I don't think I know it.'

'It's near the centre.'

My mother knew every street in Ipswich. She lived there for ten years before she married my father. But she had never heard of Blade Street. And why had the hitchhiker paused before he answered her question? Had he been making it up?

The thunder rolled over us a second time.

'*I'm going to kill you,*' Mr Rellik said.

But he said it so quietly that only I heard and this time I knew for certain. He was mad. He had escaped from Fairfields. We had picked him up in the middle of nowhere and he was going to kill us all. I leant forward, trying to catch my parents' eyes. And that was when I happened to look into the driver's mirror. That was when I saw the word that I had written on the window just a few moments before.

R E L L I K

But reflected in the mirror it said something else.

K I L L E R

What was I supposed to do? What would you do if you were in my situation? We were still doing forty miles an hour in the rain, following a long empty road with fields on one side, trees on the other and thick darkness everywhere. We were trapped inside the car with a man who could have a knife on him or even a gun or something worse. My parents didn't know anything but for some reason the man had made himself known to me. So what were my choices?

I could scream.

He would lash out and stop me before I had even opened my mouth. I could imagine those long fingers closing on my throat. He would strangle me in the back seat and my parents would drive on without even knowing what had happened. Until it was their turn.

I could trick him.

I could say I was feeling car sick. I could make them stop the car and then, when we got out, I could somehow persuade my parents to run for it. But that was a bad idea too. We were safer while we were still moving. At least Mr Rellik – or whatever his real name was – couldn't attack my father while he was driving. The car would go out of control. He couldn't reach my mother either. That would mean lunging diagonally across the car and somehow getting over the back of her seat. No. I was the only one in danger right now...but that would change the moment we stopped.

Could I talk to him? Reason with him? Hope against hope that I had imagined it all and that he didn't mean us any harm?

And then I remembered.

I was sitting behind my mother for a reason. When we had set out that morning my father had told me to sit there because there was something wrong with the door on the other side. It was an old car, a Volkswagen Estate, and the catch on one of the passenger doors had broken. My mother had said it was dangerous and had told me to sit on the left hand side and to be sure that I wore my seatbelt. I was wearing it now. But Mr Rellik wasn't.

I shifted round in my seat as if trying to get more comfortable. Mr Rellik was instantly alert. I could see that if I was going to try something I would have to move fast. He had told me who he was. He knew that I knew. He was almost expecting me to try something.

'We'll drop you off at the next roundabout,' my father said.

'That'll be fine.' But the hitchhiker had no intention of getting out at the next roundabout. His face darkened. The eye with the scar twitched. As I watched, his hand slid into his jacket and curled round something underneath the material. I didn't have to see it to know what it was. A knife. A moment later his hand reappeared and I caught the glint of silver. I knew exactly what was going to happen. He would attack me. My father would stop the car. What else could he do? Then it would be his turn. And then my mother's.

I yelled out. And then everything happened in a blur.

I had already got myself into position, curled up in the corner with my shoulders pressed into the side of the car to give me leverage. At the same time, my legs shot out. Mr Rellik had made a bad mistake. With his hand underneath his jacket he couldn't defend himself. Both my feet slammed into him, one on his shoulder, one just above his waist. I had kicked him with all my strength and as my legs uncoiled he was thrown against the opposite door.

The catch gave way. Mr Rellik didn't even have time to cry out. The door swung open and he was thrown out. Out into the night and the rain. My father must have speeded up without my noticing because we were doing almost sixty then and it seemed that the wind plucked Mr Rellik away. He hit the road in a spinning, splattering somersault. And it was worse than that. Although I hadn't seen it, an articulated lorry had been coming the other way, doing about the same speed as us. Mr Rellik fell under its front wheels. The lorry made mincemeat of him.

My mother screamed. My father stopped the car.

The articulated lorry stopped.

Suddenly everything was silent apart from the rain hammering on the roof.

My father twisted round and stared at me. The side door was still hanging open. 'What...?' he began.

Quickly I explained. I told him everything. The name on

the window. The lies Mr Rellik had told. The things he had said to me. The blood on his hand. The knife. My mother was in total shock. Her face was white and she was crying quietly. My father waited until I had finished, then he reached out and laid a hand on my arm. 'It's all right, Jacob,' he said. 'Wait here.'

He got out of the car and walked up the road. I could see him out of the back window. The lorry driver had stopped on the hard shoulder and the two of them met. There was no sign of Mr Rellik. He must have been spread out over a fair bit of the A12. It had been horrible, what had happened, but I wasn't afraid any more. I had done what I'd had to do. I'd saved both my parents and myself. We should never have stopped.

My father and the lorry driver talked for a few minutes. Then my father walked back to the car. The rain had eased off a little but he was still soaking wet.

'He's going to call the police,' my father said. 'We're nearly there so I said we'd go on. He's going to give our details to the police.'

'Did you tell him what happened?' I asked.

'Yes.' My father got back in behind the steering wheel. My mother was still crying. 'He knows you did the right thing, Jacob. Don't worry. We're going to leave now.'

We drove for another ten minutes and then, just past the first sign for Woodbridge, we turned off down a narrow lane. It twisted through woodland for about a mile and then we came to a high brick wall with spikes set along the top. We stopped in front of a pair of metal gates with an intercom system just in front. My father leant out of the car window and said something. The gates clicked and swung open automatically.

I knew where we were. We had come to Fairfields. The East Suffolk Maximum Security Hospital for the Criminally Insane.

My father had to tell them what had happened, of course. He'd agreed that with the lorry driver. This is where Mr Rellik had come from and we had just killed him. In self defence. They had to know.

I asked my father if that was why we had come here.

'Yes, Jacob,' he said. 'That's why we're here.'

We drove towards a big Victorian house with towers and barred windows and blood-red bricks. I could see how the place had got its new name though. It was surrounded by attractive gardens, the lawns spreading out for some distance underneath the high voltage searchlights. Before we had even stopped, the front door of the house opened and a bald, bearded man in a white coat came running out.

'Wait here,' my father said again.

I waited with my mother while the two of them spoke but this time I managed to hear a little of what they said.

My father did most of the talking.

'You were wrong, Dr Fielding. You were wrong. We should never have taken him...'

'None of us could have known. He was doing so well.'

'He was fine in Southwold. He was fine. I thought he was...normal. But then...this!'

'I don't know what to say to you, Mr Fisher. I don't...'

'Never again, Dr Fielding. For God's sake! Never again.'

The two men came to the car. My father leant in. 'We're going in with Dr Fielding,' he said.

'All right,' I said.

My mother didn't look up as I got out of the car. She didn't even say goodbye. That made me a little sad.

Dr Fielding put a hand on my shoulder. 'Let's go inside, Jacob,' he said. 'We have to talk about what happened.'

'All right,' I said.

Later on, they told me that the hitchhiker's name was Mr Renwick and that I had misheard him. Apparently Mr Renwick was a gardener who had been working outside Lowestoft. His car had broken down and he had managed to hitchhike as far as Southwold which was where we'd picked him up. They told me that it was mud I had seen on his wrist, not blood. And that when they had scraped him off the tarmac he had been holding not a knife but a cigarette case.

That was what they told me, but I didn't believe any of

it. After all, they also told me a lot of lies after my brother Eddy fell under that train. They even wanted me to believe that I'd pushed him! Nobody ever understood.

So here I am, back in my room, looking out of the barred window at the same old view. I had such a nice day in Southwold. I just hope I won't have to wait another nine years before they take me out again.

THE SOUND OF MURDER

i

Her name was Kate Evans. She was thirteen years old, small and slim with long, dark hair and a pale, rather serious face. She was in her last year at Brierly Hall, a prep school in Harrow-on-the-Hill, just north of London. Her best subjects were English, History and Geography but she was pretty good at anything so long as it didn't involve figures. She was popular with both the teachers and the other children. There was only one thing that made her different from everyone else at the school. Kate Evans was deaf.

It had been an accident of birth. Her mother had caught the measles while she was pregnant and the doctors had been worried even before Kate arrived in the world. They had known almost at once that something was wrong...or at least, not quite right. Kate wasn't completely deaf. She could hear some sound but speech in general was just a blur to her. The medical name for her condition was sensori-neural deafness. Part of her ear, the bit called the cochlea, wasn't working properly. She could hear a telephone ring or a dog bark but she couldn't hear a great deal else.

Kate had learned to lip-read but she didn't really need to. When she had started at Brierly Hall, she had been given a special hearing aid which fitted behind her ear and which had two settings. It could be used for day-to-day conversation. And it could also be plugged into a box, a little larger than a packet of cigarettes, which Kate carried in her top pocket. This was for use in class. Whoever was taking the lesson carried a second box, this one attached to a radio transmitter. The teacher spoke. The sound was transmitted across the room. Kate heard. It was as simple as that.

It was so simple, in fact, that Kate never thought of herself as deaf or disabled or even particularly different. The hearing aid even had certain uses. In more boring lessons – maths with Mr Thompson, for example – she could surreptitiously turn down the volume so that she no longer had to listen to him. It was also possible – if she was asked something and couldn't think of the answer – to play for time by pretending that the device was broken. Most of the teachers were too delicate to pursue the matter any further and so she nearly always got off the hook. And sometimes the machine did malfunction, with unusual results. One summer she had picked up Capital Radio which certainly livened up the day. Another time, it had been snatches of police radio communications. This had been alarming at first but the broadcasts became so interesting that soon everyone was pestering her to tell them what was going on in the fight against North London crime.

Brierly Hall wasn't a boarding school. Every afternoon Kate was picked up by the au pair, a German girl called Heidi, who spoke English that was so mangled that it was almost impossible to understand – with or without a hearing aid. Both Kate's parents worked. Her mother was a computer programmer. Her father was something to do with finance – bonds and equities and that sort of thing. She didn't have any brothers or sisters and she sometimes wondered if her parents had decided to stop having children when they had discovered that their first one wasn't perfect. She had never asked them. They were so busy, so wrapped up in their own worlds, that they never had a lot of time for her. They were kind, loving. But distant.

Kate didn't mind. She had plenty of friends. She was doing well at school. And at the start of her last year – the Christmas term – at Brierly Hall, she was definitely enjoying life.

But that was the term that the new French teacher, Mr Spencer, arrived. And it was with the coming of Mr Spencer that the whole nightmare began.

ii

To start with, he looked just like all the other teachers who had chosen to lock themselves away in the secluded world of Brierly Hall. He wasn't exactly young any more but nor was he particularly old. He seemed to be stuck somewhere in between. He was wearing an old-fashioned sports jacket, corduroy trousers, white shirt, tie (striped, of course) and V-necked jersey. All of his clothes looked well lived-in. He had dark eyes, dark, curly hair and a beard. Although he was a physically large man, there was something about him that made him look beaten down, defeated. His shoulders were hunched. His eyes blinked frequently. He didn't smile.

Kate saw him on the first day of term. She was walking down the corridor with her best friend, a boy called Martin White. He and Kate were just passing the staff room when the door opened and the new teacher came out and hurried past them on his way to class. He didn't speak to them but his arm briefly touched Kate's shoulder and it was then, at that moment of contact, that it happened.

Kate's hearing aid malfunctioned. There was a loud whistling in her ear; so loud that she actually recoiled, her hand stretching out and her face contorting. The sound cut right through her head. She could feel it even after it was gone.

'What is it?' Martin asked. He had seen Kate double up.

'Feedback.' Kate took a deep breath. Fortunately, it seemed to be over. She tapped at her ear. 'I've never had it so loud. Just my luck if my hearing aid's playing up on the first day of term.' She looked back at the new teacher who was just disappearing through a set of double doors. 'Who's that?'

'I think it must be Mr Spencer. Or Monsieur Spen-saire, perhaps, I should say.'

'The new French teacher.'

'Oui, oui!' Martin sniffed. 'He looks even more boring than the last one.'

Their old French teacher, Mr Silberman, had announced his retirement the term before – much to the relief of almost everybody. He must have been at least eighty years old and was one of the only teachers who regularly fell asleep in his own lessons. Kate had been hoping for a younger, sexier replacement. Her first sighting had left her distinctly disappointed.

And it was strange the way her hearing aid had reacted when he touched her. That piercing feedback. It was almost as if...

No. She put the thought out of her mind. Mr Spencer hadn't caused the problem. It had simply happened when he walked past.

She met the new teacher for a second time that afternoon. French was the last lesson of the day. Mr

Spencer had taken over Mr Silberman's old classroom and had already removed the posters showing the different varieties of French cheese, which at least proved he had a bit of sense. But as he took their names, handed out the new exercise books and did all the things that teachers always do on the first day of term, he seemed about as cheerful and lively as a French dictionary. He even forced them to sit in alphabetical order. Mr Silberman had never done that.

He was, of course, wearing the radio transmitter that allowed Kate to hear him. He had slipped the box into his top pocket and clipped the microphone to his tie. But throughout the lesson, the machine malfunctioned with a series of hisses, bleeps and squawking noises that had Kate reeling. She was relieved when the final bell went even if it added to the headache she'd already got. It was about the only thing she heard properly.

She was the first to stand up and was already making her way to the door when Mr Spencer spoke. There were just two words but this time she heard him quite clearly. She stopped dead in her tracks. She was certain the words were addressed to her.

'Rotten cow!'

Kate turned round. She was blushing – though whether with embarrassment or anger she wasn't sure. Mr Spencer was standing at his desk clutching a pile of books. For the first time she noticed that the backs of his hands were covered in dark hair. 'I'm sorry, sir?' she said.

He looked up. 'What is it, Kate?' he asked. He knew her name. But of course, new teachers always remembered her name first.

'What did you say?' Kate asked. She was aware that she sounded angry. Everyone had stopped what they were doing. They were all looking at her.

'I didn't say anything,' Mr Spencer said. He smiled at her. 'Did you hear everything all right during the lesson, Kate? I did mean to ask...'

'Yes...' Kate stammered, suddenly unsure of herself. Could she have misheard him? Or had the two words come from somewhere else – like the radio or the police reports? But no...

'Rotten cow.'

She had heard him. It had been his voice.

'I'll see you tomorrow, then.' Mr Spencer was still smiling. The smile changed his face. He looked a whole lot more human.

Kate turned and left the class.

iii

The next day, the problems with the hearing aid were even worse. And it wasn't just the distortions. While Mr Spencer took the class through a fairly simple comprehension test, all Kate heard was a barrage of swear-words. They came into her ear from nowhere. Nasty, jabbing words that she would never have dreamed of using herself. She remembered how she had picked up Capital Radio the summer before and wondered if the same thing wasn't happening again. But these words weren't out of any radio programme. Nobody would be allowed to say things like this on the air.

She did the best she could with the comprehension, but knew that she'd missed at least half of it and probably mistranslated the rest. She handed in her paper with a heavy heart, and as her fingertips approached those of Mr Spencer she was rewarded with another scream of static and interference. She wondered how she would get through the rest of the day.

And yet the strange thing was that, after French, the hearing aid worked perfectly. She had no problems in Maths or History and it was only in the corridor just before lunch that the receiver started playing up once again. Even as she felt the hiss rising up in her eardrums, Kate was turning round. And sure enough, there he was. Mr Spencer was ambling into the staff room, his hands in his pockets, his shoulders hunched. She watched the door close. The hissing stopped.

That afternoon, after lunch, she told Martin what had happened. Martin was a good-looking thirteen-year-old with blue eyes and straw-coloured hair which hung in his eyes. He was always first in games but even his best friends had to agree that he wasn't particularly bright. For a long minute he thought about what Kate had said. 'Are you telling me,' he said, 'that there's something about Mr Spencer that sets off your hearing aid? That he's... like...transmitting signals or something?'

'That's exactly what I'm saying,' Kate replied. 'But it's never happened to me before. I wouldn't have said it was possible!'

'I did once hear about this man who kept on hearing concerts,' Martin said. 'I mean, he got voices and operas and classical music in his head and it was driving him mad. He was going to commit suicide. But then they found he had a filling in his back tooth and it was picking up Radio Three.'

'What's that got to do with anything?' Kate asked.

Martin shrugged. 'I was just trying to be helpful.'

The afternoon seemed to stretch on for ever. Kate didn't have any more French lessons and she didn't get any more interference but even so she found it hard to concentrate. It was like being on some sort of ghost train. As each minute ticked by she was expecting something to jump out at her – a swear-word, another electronic scream. By the end of the day her nerves were in tatters and she decided she'd have to talk it over with her parents. She was beginning to feel almost nervous. She couldn't understand it but she was becoming afraid.

Heidi came for her at four o'clock. The German au pair was always smiling and friendly but sometimes Kate suspected that she didn't understand a single word. She drove a red Nissan and Kate was just about to get in when a single faint whine in her ear made her stop and turn round, already knowing what she would see.

And there he was. Mr Spencer had just come out of the school with a pile of books under his arm. He was walking towards a waiting VW Golf and as he reached it he must have stumbled because suddenly all the books slipped from under his arm and fell to the ground. At once the door of the Golf opened and a woman got out. It had to be Mrs Spencer; a thin, bony woman with hair between brown and grey tied tightly behind her head. Everything about her was tight. Her clothes – an Arran jersey and jeans. Her eyes. The way she moved.

She was saying something to her husband and he seemed to be apologising. They were too far away for Kate to be able to hear but she found herself doing something she had been told she should never do, something she knew was wrong. She lip-read the conversation.

'...so clumsy! Just get a move on, George. I haven't got all day.'

'Yes, dear. Sorry, dear.'

'You're a complete waste of time! A boring little man in

a boring little job. Have you got them all?'

'I think so, dear.'

Kate blinked and looked away, immediately guilty about eavesdropping. But even without sound, even from this distance, she had been able to detect the venom in the woman's voice. And once again she thought about the two words she had heard in the French lesson.

'Rotten cow...'

'Are you now coming, please, Katie?' Heidi called out to her in her sing-song voice.

Kate watched Mr and Mrs Spencer drive away. Then she got in next to the au pair.

She wanted to talk to her parents that evening but when she got home, there was a note on the kitchen table. They'd gone out to dinner and wouldn't be home until late. She went to bed with her own thoughts and that same, nudging sense of fear.

iv

Nothing more happened for about a week. The evenings got darker and the weather got worse. The interference continued but Kate got used to turning the transmitter off during French lessons. If she was reading or writing, she didn't need it, and she could lip-read...even though it was next to impossible in French. It was when they had oral work that she was forced to turn the thing back on and put up with whatever came her way. And it was during one of those lessons that the voice came again.

They were reading a book, each taking it in turns to read the words out in French and then to translate them. It was Kate's turn. She was standing with the book open in front of her.

'Bonne-Maman arrivait toujours en taxi et ne donnait jamais de pourboire au chauffeur,' she read.

Mr Spencer looked at her with his watery, dark eyes. *'I'm going to kill her,'* he said.

Kate faltered, then went on. 'Elle était petite…'

'I'm going to kill her…'

'…et paraissait rapetisser un peu plus chaque année.'

'Nobody will know.'

'Elle avait des cheveux…' Kate was suddenly aware that everyone was looking at her. One or two of the other girls were giggling. She stopped, blushing without quite knowing why. There was a whine in her ear. She waited until it had died away.

'Didn't you hear me, Kate?' Mr Spencer asked. He was staring at her, puzzled.

'I'm sorry, sir?' Kate sat down. The classroom was beginning to spin slowly around her and she wondered if she was going to faint.

'I asked you to translate.'

'Oh. Right.' Kate tried to concentrate on the book.

'I'm going to murder her!'

'Murder?' Kate repeated the word. At least, the word slipped out of her lips before she could stop it.

Something glimmered in the French teacher's eyes. 'What did you say?' he demanded.

'Mother...I mean grandmother!' Kate gazed at the black and white pages of the book, trying to bury herself in them. 'Grandma always came by taxi,' she began. 'And she never gave the driver...she never gave the driver...' She had stumbled on a word.

'Pourboire,' Mr Spencer said. *'I'm going to murder her tonight.'*

Hands were going up around the class. He had asked them if they knew the word 'pourboire'. That was what he had said. But that wasn't what Kate had heard.

'With a kitchen knife.'

'Does it mean "a drink", sir?'

'No.'

'A tip?'

'Yes. Well done, Nicholas. *I'm going to stab her with a kitchen knife. Nobody will know.'*

Kate got to her feet. She had knocked her chair over behind her. 'I'm sorry,' she said. 'I don't feel well.'

She ran out of the room.

V

The matron said it was flu. But the matron always said everything was flu. There was a joke in the school that if you went to the matron with both your legs chopped off and a spear in your neck, she'd give you half a disprin and tell you to come back the next day. Fortunately, it was a Friday afternoon. The matron told Kate to have plenty of rest over the weekend and to stay indoors. She didn't even give her the half disprin.

Kate did two things that weekend.

The first was to visit her doctor and arrange for a new hearing aid to be sent to her. But somehow she knew she was wasting her time. The hearing aid worked in every lesson except French. It worked at home and it worked at the doctor's. Try as she might, Kate couldn't think of any reason why it should play up when she was close to Mr Spencer. Could there be something in Martin's ridiculous story about the filling? Could Mr Spencer have a false tooth or something that was interfering with the signal? But, no. Kate knew that she was dealing with something different, something that had no easy explanation. She kept on thinking about what she had heard. The words had been so vicious, and so deliberate. They echoed in her head, even when she was asleep. The worst thing was, she still wasn't sure where they had come from. They couldn't have come from Mr Spencer himself. She had never actually seen them cross his lips.

And so, on Sunday, she tried to tell her mother what had happened. Tried and failed. It was a bad time of the year for Caroline Evans. She had just set up a complicated computer system for a chain of organic supermarkets. As always, there were teething problems and the moment anything went wrong she was the one who got the blame. When Kate came into the sitting room after breakfast, her mother was already in a bad mood. The fax had been spitting out pages all morning. Mangoes in Manchester and leeks that had failed to arrive in Leeds.

'Mum…'

Caroline Evans looked up from her lap-top, a cigarette halfway to her lips. She always smoked when a new system was coming on-line. The rest of the year she spent trying to give up. 'Yes, darling?'

'I need to talk to you about something that's happening at school.'

'What is it?' Caroline was genuinely concerned. That was the thing about her. She did worry about Kate – when she had time.

'It's this teacher. And my hearing aid…' Kate began but then the telephone rang and it was the IT manager from the supermarket and suddenly the conversation was all bytes and modules and ten minutes later Caroline was still arguing down the line.

At last she hung up. 'I'm sorry, darling,' she said. 'Now what was it about this teacher?'

'It doesn't matter,' Kate said. She had decided. She would handle this on her own.

And on Monday, she went back to school with the same resolve. There was a simple solution to her problem. She would talk to Mr Spencer himself! She would explain the problem to him and between them they would work out what was causing it.

But Mr Spencer wasn't at school on Monday.

As soon as she arrived she knew something was wrong. The first lesson had been cancelled and instead there was to be an assembly in the school theatre. She saw one or two of the teachers looking shaken and upset. As she made her way across the schoolyard, Martin hurried up to her. 'Have you heard?' he whispered. But before he could tell her, Miss Primrose, the music teacher, had stepped between them and Martin could say no more.

There were three hundred and twenty children at Brierly Hall and it was a tight squeeze inside the theatre. They sat, shoulder to shoulder, while the staff took their places on the stage. Then the head teacher appeared. His name was Mr Fellner and normally he was a lively, humorous man. It was said that he was the most popular head that Brierly Hall had ever had. But today he was grim-faced and serious.

'I'm afraid I have some bad news for you,' he said and there was something about the tone of his voice that made everyone know that he was about to tell them the very worst news possible. 'I would have preferred to tell your parents before I tell you, but unfortunately that won't be possible because it will be on the television news tonight and I would prefer you to hear it from me first.' He paused. 'As some of you may have already noticed, Mr Spencer is not with us today. The reason for this is that something awful has happened. His wife has died.

'You may be wondering why this should be on the news. Well, I spoke to the police this morning and although it's a very shocking thing and I'm sure many of you will want to talk about this with your form teachers after this assembly, it would appear that Mrs Spencer has been murdered.'

A whisper that quickly rose into an excited buzz zigzagged its way through the rows of children but for Kate it was as if she had been snatched out of her seat and sent spinning into outer space. Murdered!

'I'm going to kill her!'

It wasn't possible. Murders happened in books and in television programmes. You read about murders in the newspapers or heard about them on the news.

'I'm going to murder her!'

The voice had told her it was going to happen. It had warned her. And she had refused to listen.

'There is no need for any of you to be afraid,' Mr Fellner was saying. 'Geraldine Spencer lived in Stanmore, which is quite a long way from here. As far as we know, from what the police have told us, she was attacked while she was out walking on Stanmore Common. She was attacked…'

'With a kitchen knife.'

'…with some sort of knife. Possibly it was somebody wanting to rob her. I will of course give you further information when I have it.

'But right now I think it would be appropriate if we put our hands together and prayed. Mr Spencer has only been with the school for a short time but even so he is still part of the family, here at Brierly Hall. I spoke to him on the telephone briefly this morning and of course he's completely devastated. He'll be away for the next few weeks at least, possibly until the end of term, but I'm sure it would be of comfort for him to know that our thoughts are with him. Let's start with the Lord's Prayer…'

And the school prayed. But not Kate.

She was sick, frightened, confused. A whirl of images flashed through her mind. There was Mr Spencer, walking down the corridor for the first time. There were his hands with the dark hair reaching almost to his fingers. And again, outside the school, dropping the books while the woman waited for him in his car. With a thrill, Kate realised that she had actually seen Mrs Spencer, the wife who was now dead, killed with a knife while she was walking in the park. The two of them hadn't seemed very happy at the time. How could they have known that it was going to be one of their last days together?

How could they have known?

Could they have known?

Could one of them have known?

Kate fainted – and that was something else she thought only happened in television plays. The room took one lurching spin around her and then jerked away as she collapsed off her chair and on to the floor. Later on, of course, the other children would tease her. Trust a girl to faint just because there'd been a murder. But of course, none of them understood.

Mr Spencer had murdered his wife. And only Kate knew.

vi

Strangely enough, it was Martin who first mentioned the word telepathy. Martin didn't have that many four-syllable words in his vocabulary.

He was talking to Kate the next day, the day after they had all heard the big announcement. By this time, the murder had indeed been reported on the television news and had also appeared in all the newspapers. Most of them had carried photographs of Geraldine Spencer and there had been pictures of George Spencer too in the *Daily Mail* and the *Telegraph*. At school, of course, nobody had talked about anything else and it was getting harder and harder to distinguish facts from gossip, gossip from rumour and rumour from fantastic lies.

But Kate knew this much.

Geraldine Spencer had been stabbed at four o'clock on Saturday afternoon while she was walking her dog, a poodle, on Stanmore Common. The police hadn't yet found the murder weapon. According to the Detective Inspector who was leading the enquiry, this would be a vital clue if it ever turned up. There had been no witnesses. Geraldine Spencer had been forty-two years old and had been married to George Spencer for seventeen years. There were no children. Surprisingly, Mrs Spencer was a wealthy woman. It turned out that her father had run a chain of hotels and she had inherited a lot of money a few years before. All this money would go to her husband.

George Spencer was the prime suspect in the murder. He had been interviewed by the police…once, or several times. It depended whom you believed. But it seemed that he had an alibi. He had been at the cinema that afternoon. Without the murder weapon, there was absolutely no evidence against him. He was now at home.

Alex Burford, who was in Kate's class and who actually lived near Stanmore, said that his mother had seen Mr Spencer at the funeral, sobbing uncontrollably and at one point even trying to throw himself into his wife's grave. But nearly everything Alex said was untrue and nobody believed him now.

Although Kate had been teased non-stop for fainting during the assembly, she had said nothing. At least, not the first day. But by the end of the second she'd had enough and after the last lesson she'd taken Martin to one side and described everything that had happened – not because she thought he could help but because she simply had to get it off her chest.

At least Martin hadn't laughed at her. Nor had he refused to believe her. He had listened in silence, scratched his head, and then finally given his opinion.

'This voice you heard,' he said. 'If it wasn't the radio and it wasn't what he was saying, you don't think it could have been…sort of, what he was thinking? Like telepathy or something?'

'Telepathy?'

'I saw this programme on television once. It was about that man who can bend spoons and stuff. Anyway, he did this trick where someone drew a picture on a sheet of paper and sealed it in an envelope. And then he drew the same picture. He said he could read the other person's mind. He actually did it! Because he was telepathic.'

'But Martin! I can't read people's minds!'

'No. I know. But maybe it's something to do with…I don't know. But the moment you met him you said your hearing aid went all screwy. So maybe for some reason you can't hear what he says but you can hear what he thinks.'

'That's crazy…' Kate regretted the words the moment they were spoken. Martin looked glum and she realised she'd offended him. Martin knew he was thick. He'd often said as much. But he didn't like it when people treated him as if he was thick. She reached out and put a hand on his arm. 'I mean, it sounds crazy. But…I don't know…!'

And the more she thought about it, the more she began to wonder if Martin hadn't somehow stumbled on the truth.

George Spencer didn't love his wife. That much Kate knew from the brief sight she had had of them together. The voice had said he was going to murder her, stab her with a kitchen knife. And that was what had happened. Martin was right. The hearing aid only ever played up when Mr Spencer was near. So maybe, impossibly, it had transmitted…

…not what he was saying.

What he was thinking.

Kate lifted the receiver out of her top pocket and stared at it. The little silver box seemed so small, so ordinary. Although she depended on it every day of her life, she had never really given it much thought. It was just a machine.

Martin stood up suddenly. He had seen his mother draw up in her BMW convertible. Martin's parents were divorced and as he often liked to tell Kate, his mum had got the house, the car, the money…everything, including him!

'You know,' he muttered, 'I hope for you're sake you're not telepathic.'

'What do you mean?' Kate asked.

'Well, if Mr Spencer did bump off his wife, and you know what he's thinking, what are you going to do when he comes back?'

vii

Mr Spencer came back two weeks before the end of term. The head teacher made another speech at assembly the day before he arrived.

'Mr Spencer has asked to come back before the end of term because he wants his life to return to normal as soon as possible and I am sure that all of us here at Brierly Hall will do everything we can to help him. As I'm sure you all know, the police have been unable to find the wicked person who attacked and killed Geraldine Spencer. Mr Spencer has of course been questioned about the death of his wife but it's important that you understand that this is entirely normal in an investigation of this sort and that there is no question that he was in any way involved. I must ask you, all of you, to be kind and to be sympathetic. Christmas is just a few weeks away. Let's look forward to that and put this whole dreadful business behind us.'

And there he was, suddenly, almost as if he had never been away. Mr Spencer was thinner and some people said there was a touch more grey in his hair. He walked more slowly and when he spoke there was a softness, even a sadness, in his voice that hadn't been there before. There was one other thing that was different about him. He had bought himself new clothes; a new jacket and black shiny shoes that squeaked a little when he walked.

For Kate, French was the first lesson of the day – and she was dreading it. As she streamed into the classroom with the other children, she saw Martin holding one hand up, two fingers crossed. Even now, she wasn't sure if he really had taken her seriously. Martin loved science fiction and Marvel comic books and Kate sometimes wondered if he knew where real life ended and fantasy began. Everyone took their seats. Mr Spencer was standing at the blackboard, writing out the conditional tense of 'aimer'. He turned round and spoke to them.

'I got away with it. I killed the old cow, and the police couldn't touch me!'

Sitting in the front row, Kate let out a stifled cry. The teacher's dark eyes were suddenly on her.

'What is it, Kate?

'Nothing, sir.'

'I've got her money. I'm rich! And I'm free of her.' The hearing aid whined.

Kate writhed in her seat. Everyone was looking at her. Mr Spencer too. She could see the puzzlement in his face. Worse, she could hear it.

'That girl again! What's wrong with her? Does she know something? No! That's not possible. But why is she looking at me like that?'

Kate forced herself to look away.

'She's looking away! It's almost as if she knows what I'm thinking! No. Don't be stupid. She doesn't know anything. The police don't know anything. The knife! They haven't found the knife. They'll never find the knife.'

Kate couldn't bear it any more. The hearing aid was screaming and buzzing in her ear. She opened her exercise book and buried herself in it, hoping that if she concentrated enough on the words, she could make the voice go away.

And it worked. Her head was still filled with interference but somewhere, in the distance, she could hear Mr Spencer walking across the room – squeak, squeak, squeak. The sound of his new shoes was one thing that transmitted perfectly. Now he was talking to the rest of the class. 'The conditional tense is formed by taking the infinitive, 'aimer', and adding…'

Somehow she made it to the end of the lesson although it was the longest fifty minutes of her life. At last the bell went, followed by the usual shuffling of books and slamming of desks.

'I will see you tomorrow,' Mr Spencer called out over the din. Then… 'Kate! Can I have a word with you, please?'

Kate stopped dead in her tracks. She glanced despairingly at Martin who shrugged helplessly, already on his way out. For a moment she was tempted to run. But that was ridiculous. Where would she go? She forced herself not to panic. There was nothing Mr Spencer could do. Not here, in school, in the middle of the day. She turned round slowly and looked at the teacher who was sitting by his desk. The hearing aid crackled. She walked over to him. Suddenly there were only two of them in the room.

'Is something the matter?' Mr Spencer asked.

'What do you know? How do you know? I killed Dina! Killed my wife! Stabbed her with a knife.'

'Nothing's the matter, sir,' Kate said. She had to concentrate. Listen to the first voice. Ignore the second.

'You were behaving very strangely in my class.'

'They can't find the knife. I've got the knife.'

'My hearing aid…it's…it's not working,' Kate said. She

was begging him to stop. She didn't want to know.

'*It's in the spare locker.*'

'You should get it seen to,' Mr Spencer said.

'Yes, sir.'

'*In the spare locker. In the spare locker. Nobody will look there. Nobody knows.*'

Mr Spencer was staring at her now, as if he were trying to see inside her head. Kate forced herself to look ordinary, to pretend that nothing was happening. He was suspicious. She knew it. She had to make him trust her.

'I was very sorry, sir,' she stammered. 'I mean, we were all very sorry about what happened to Dina. I'm sure the police will find who did it. You must be very sad.'

'I am very sad,' Mr Spencer said. But then he frowned. 'Why did you call her Dina?' he asked.

The hearing aid was howling.

'I thought that was her name,' Kate said.

'Her name was Geraldine. I used to call her Dina, though. But I'll tell you something very strange, Kate. I was the only person who called her that. And nobody else knew. It was a private name.'

'I thought…'

'What did you think, Kate? How did you know that name?'

'I just thought it was her name, sir.'

Mr Spencer's eyes went blank and for the first time the

noise in Kate's head stopped. He stood up and, despite herself, Kate took a step back. She was afraid of him. And he knew it. It was obvious.

'Make sure you get your hearing aid seen to, Kate,' Mr Spencer said. 'We don't want you missing any French.'

'Yes, sir.'

'All right. You can go.'

Relieved, she gathered up her things and walked over to the door, but just as she was about to leave, he called out to her.

'Stop, Kate. There's something I want to say.'

'Yes, sir?' She stopped and turned round.

And knew that he had tricked her.

Mr Spencer hadn't said anything at all. He had thought it. As crazy as his suspicions had been, he had decided to put them to the test. And now he knew.

Kate opened her mouth to speak but she could see the sudden flare of cruelty in those dark eyes and knew that Geraldine Spencer would have seen exactly the same before the knife sliced into her.

She ran through the door and down the corridor, never once stopping to look behind.

viii

What could she do?

She could go to Mr Fellner. But she knew that the head

teacher would never believe her. The main difference between adults and children isn't that adults are older, bigger, smarter or more experienced. It's that they don't believe. Adults always have to find explanations for everything and Kate knew that if she went to Mr Fellner he would think she was either hysterical or crazy but he certainly wouldn't believe her.

She could go to her parents. But that wasn't easy. Her father was at some bank in Zurich for three days. Her mother had gone to visit a new client in Edinburgh and wouldn't be home until the weekend. That left Heidi but it would be a day's work just to get the au pair to understand what she was saying and even then Kate doubted there would be anything she could do.

Could she telephone the police? No. The police were adults too. At best they would treat the telephone call as some cruel sort of hoax. The fact was that, apart from Martin, there was probably no one in the world who would believe her story of...telepathy or whatever it was. She still wasn't sure that she believed it herself.

'The trouble is, you've got no proof,' Martin said. During lunch she had told him what had happened and once again he had surprised her. He hadn't questioned a word of what she had said. And once again he was right.

'Proof?'

'It's your word against his. And if you go to the police talking about telepathy and that sort of thing, they'll think you're raving mad.'

'I'm not the mad one!' Kate remembered the look in Mr Spencer's eyes and shivered.

'What about the knife?'

'What about it?' Kate didn't even want to think about it.

'You know where it is!'

It was in the locker. That was what Mr Spencer had said – or thought.

Brierly Hall had been around for about a hundred and fifty years. Even in Victorian times it had been a school. Of course, most of it had been rebuilt more recently than that. The more successful the school had become, the more money it had attracted, and in the Eighties and Nineties they'd built the theatre, the music wing, three new classrooms and a heated swimming pool. But the core of the school was old. The central building (A Block) belonged to another century with thick, tile-covered walls, bare wooden floors, arched windows and – in the basement – a series of dusty rooms and passageways containing hot water tanks, heating systems and generators. The dining hall and the head teacher's study were in A Block. So was the staff room. And on the other side of the staff room there was a row of wooden lockers, one for every teacher in the school.

'It's in the spare locker.'

'I bet it's got his fingerprints on it,' Martin said. 'And bits of his wife's blood…'

'Shut up, Martin!' Kate didn't want to hear this.

But Martin went on, excited. 'If you got the knife, they'd have to believe you. It wouldn't even matter how you found it. Didn't you read what the police said? They said it was a vital clue.'

'Yes! But how am I supposed to get it?' Kate asked, miserably. 'The lockers are next to the staff room and we're not allowed anywhere near them.'

'You could sneak in…'

'With everyone there?'

'You could do it after school.'

'When?'

'Today! I'll help you. We could do it together.'

'But if Mr Spencer knows that I know about the knife…'

'He won't know!' Martin said. 'I mean, you only know because you heard him thinking about it. But how could he know that he was thinking about it just then? If you get the knife, then you've got the proof. And if you've got the proof, you can go to the police…'

'I'm not sure,' Kate sighed. 'What happens if someone sees us? And it'll be dark…'

'It'll only take us two minutes.' Martin smiled and Kate saw that to him this was just some crazy adventure, something to boast about afterwards. It was different for her. She had been inside Mr Spencer's head. She knew what was there.

'You promise you'll stay with me?' Kate said.

'I promise!'

'OK.' There were games that afternoon and naturally the two of them were in different teams. 'I'll meet you round by the toilets. At a quarter to four.'

'I'll be there.'

ix

He wasn't there, of course. It should have been easy. But everything went wrong.

Later that day, Kate found herself watching the last of the children pour out of the school and into the waiting cars. After lunch, she had telephoned Heidi and told her that she was going to be late. Heidi had agreed to come at four thirty. 'Halb funf'. Kate had translated it to be sure. She looked at her watch. It was already ten to four. But there was no sign of Martin.

There was a movement close by and she saw another of the boys, Sam Twivey, hurrying past, late as usual. She called out to him. 'Sam?'

The other boy saw her and stopped.

'Have you seen Martin?'

'Didn't you hear? He got hurt playing football.'

'What?'

'Someone kicked him in the…you-know-where. He got carried off. His mum came for him and he went home.' The boy looked away into the gloom. 'My dad's here. I've got to go…'

So she was on her own.

The sensible thing, of course, would have been to have gone. To have left the school and gone home. It was dark and there were a few wisps of fog in the air, hanging across the road, a screen that cut her off from the world outside Brierly Hall. As far as she could tell, all the teachers had left. She was completely on her own. Heidi wouldn't be here for another twenty-five minutes. It was cold. She would be better off waiting inside…that was what she told herself. But even as she turned round and walked back into A Block, she knew what she was going to do. She had to find the knife.

She simply couldn't stand any more. Waiting for French lessons, wondering what she was going to hear. She wanted the whole thing to be over with and, with or without Martin, she was going to do it now. Find the knife. Take it to the police. Tell them her story. Whether they believed her or not, they would have the evidence in front of them. They would have to act.

It was strange, walking through the school on her own. Normally the corridors would be full of movement and colour, children hurtling from class to class, doors swinging open and shut. Empty, everything was different. The ceilings felt higher. The corridors felt longer. The photographs of teachers and old boys on the walls were suddenly ghost-like and Kate shivered. Many of these pictures had been taken decades ago. Many of the black and white faces watching her as she tiptoed back towards the staff room would indeed belong to the dead.

She reached a set of swing doors. The emptiness had made them bigger and heavier and she felt she was using all her strength to open them. It was as if they didn't want her to pass through. Something moved. She stopped and twisted round expecting to see someone behind her but there was nobody in the corridor. Just shadows creeping in on her from all sides.

This was stupid. This was a mistake. But it was too late. She was almost there. She might as well get it over with.

She opened the door of the staff room. Children were never allowed in here, not at any time and Kate felt a twinge of guilt as she crossed the threshold and went in. The room was so shabby and untidy. Half the armchairs were worn out (a bit like some of the people who sat in them, she thought). She could smell cigarette smoke even though the head teacher was always lecturing them about the dangers of smoking. It was like going backstage in a magic show. Or peeking into the kitchen of a smart restaurant. This was a side of the school that Kate wasn't meant to see.

She went through as quickly as she could. The passage with the lockers was on the other side. It connected the staff room with another exit which was only used during fire drills. That was how Kate knew where the lockers were. She wished now that she had thought to bring a torch. There were only two windows and they were high up. The fog, pale and white, nuzzled against the glass. Little light came in.

Eighteen lockers, gnarled and wooden, stood shoulder to shoulder along one wall. Fourteen of them were in use. Each of these had a rectangle of white cardboard with a name written in black letters. ELLIS, THOMPSON, STANDRING, PRIESTMAN… Padlocks of different shapes and sizes, some with keys, some with combinations, fastened the doors. The four lockers at the very end of the corridor were unmarked. One of them had a broken hinge and a door hanging off at an angle. Spare lockers. This was what Mr Spencer had been thinking about. This was where he had hidden the knife.

The first locker was empty. The second, the one with the broken door, contained a pile of mouldy books. Kate opened the third locker and jerked back as a spider, brown and hairy, scurried out and across the floor. That just left one locker, the furthest one away. She reached out for the door and pulled it open. There was a bundle of what looked like old clothes thrown into the corner. Was there something wrapped inside? She reached in.

Her hearing aid exploded into life inside her ear.

A hand touched her shoulder.

'Are you looking for this?' Mr Spencer said.

Kate jerked round and fell back against the wall, shock and disbelief coursing through her. The French teacher was hovering over her, his eyes glistening in the dim evening light, his lips drawn back. There was a kitchen knife in his hand.

'I wondered if you'd come,' he whispered. 'I couldn't be sure. In the classroom. But somehow I knew you'd found out. You knew about the knife! How did you do it, Kate? Can you read my mind?'

'I have to kill her…'

'Do you know what I'm thinking now?'

Kate tried to speak but the words wouldn't come. She couldn't move. Sheer terror had swept away all her strength. She forced herself to take a breath. 'You killed your wife…'

Mr Spencer nodded. He was sweating. She could see globs of perspiration on his forehead. A trickle of sweat snaked down the side of his face. When he spoke, his voice was low, the words tumbling out one after another. 'Yes. I killed her. You're just a child. You don't understand.

That woman! Always nagging me. I was never good enough for her. She never left me alone. Seventeen years of it! No children. No love. She enjoyed being cruel to me. But I couldn't divorce her. It was her house. Her money. She'd have taken everything. And every day, she went on and on and on at me. I hated her. And in the end I couldn't bear it any more...'

'I have to kill her. She mustn't tell...'

Kate could hear what he was thinking. The words were as clear as the ones he was speaking. She had to distract him. Play for time. Keep him talking. Someone would come...

'Why did you hide the knife here?' she asked.

'I had to put it somewhere! The murder weapon. They're clever...the police. They'd know it was mine. I couldn't dump it. It would be found. So I hid it. Not in my locker. They looked there. I knew they would.' He smiled. Saliva was flecking his lips, hanging in the tangle of his beard. 'But in the old locker. Under those clothes. Nobody thought of that.

'Except you. Did you read my mind? Are you reading my mind now?'

'You can't do anything to me,' Kate began.

'Yes, I can.'

'I told lots of people about you. My mum and dad...'

'She's lying.'

'If you hurt me, people will know…'

And then Kate saw it. Not words this time. Pictures. The horrible pictures that were inside Mr Spencer's head. The knife stabbing forward. Going into her. He was going to kill her because he had decided he had no choice. She would disappear and maybe he would get away with it. What did it matter anyway? He was already a murderer. One more death would make no difference.

She saw his thoughts. She saw him draw back the knife a second before he actually did it. And that was what saved her. She screamed and threw herself forward, into him. He was caught off balance. Half a second later and the knife would have been swinging towards her but she had been that half second ahead of him. Somehow Kate managed to scramble to her feet and then she was away, back down the corridor and into the staff room, knowing that Mr Spencer was only inches behind.

'Come back! Kill her! Little brat! Die!'

The words shuddered through her hearing aid and into her skull. Static howled and hissed. Blind with panic, Kate stumbled through the empty staff room, crashing into a table and almost losing her balance. Her hand flailed out and caught hold of an upright lamp, standing near the door. She jerked and pulled it down behind her. The lamp hit Mr Spencer, the wire tangling around his feet. She heard him cry out and fall. And then she had reached the door. She slammed it behind her, wishing it had a key that she could turn. Without stopping to draw breath, she headed off down the corridor, hurtling into the darkness of the deserted school.

She had gone the wrong way. She felt the wind on the back of her neck as the door crashed open behind her and knew that she should have headed back towards the exit and out into the street. Ahead of her was the dining room, the secretary's office, stairs going up to classrooms and down to the basement. Which way now? She threw open the door of the dining room. Long rows of empty tables stretched down with the hatchways into the kitchen beyond them. No. Not that way. She'd be trapped. She left the door open, thinking she could fool Mr Spencer into thinking she'd gone in. Instead she took the stairs. Up or down? Down was faster. But that was a mistake too. The stairs led to the basement. Another dead end.

'Where is she? Where is she? Where is she?'

She could only just hear what he was thinking. He had slowed down. He must still be in the upstairs corridor.

'In here...?'

Kate froze. Mr Spencer was outside the dining room. He was looking in through the empty door. And maybe because the school was empty, maybe because there were no distractions, it wasn't just his thoughts that were being transmitted to her. She could also see with his eyes.

'Listen? Nothing! Is she in here? No. She wouldn't go in here. But she can't be far. Find her. Kill her. Cut her throat and bury her. No-one will know.'

Kate took a couple of steps forward.

She could see nothing. Nothing at all. She had only ever been in the basement once…she had gone down there as a dare. She remembered a long, low-ceilinged room with archways leading off it, a bit like a wine cellar. There were machines. She could feel them humming now. A bank of electric generators on one side and a tangle of wires and pipes. It was very warm in the basement. There were heating systems too. She wanted to turn the light on but knew that she couldn't. That would bring him to her. And there was no way out.

Somewhere, above her, she heard a floorboard creak. No. She couldn't have heard it. But Mr Spencer had. She was hearing with his ears! He had reached the stairs.

'Where is she? Did she go up? Upstairs…'

Another creak. He had taken the stairs. He was climbing up. Kate swayed in the darkness, almost faint with relief. But then he stopped.

'No! I'd have heard her! No carpet on the stairs. If she'd gone up, I'd have heard her. She must have gone down.'

She heard him turn. Heard him come down.

Kate was petrified. In Science class she'd once seen a bug, millions of years old, caught in a piece of amber. That was how she felt now. The inky darkness was crushing her. She couldn't breathe.

Squeak. Squeak. Squeak. The French teacher, wearing his new shoes, moved slowly down the stairs. Kate backed away. Her left hand touched a wall and there was a clink as her watch came into contact with something, metal against metal. The sound was tiny. But he'd heard it.

'She's here. Where's the light? I can't find the light. Wait…'

He found a switch outside in the corridor and turned it on. Yellow light spilled in through a doorway, only reaching halfway into the chamber. Kate squeezed herself backwards. She was between two bulky machines. Thick cables pressed against her back. The air smelt of hot metal. She tried to make herself as small as she could. What was Mr Spencer doing? Kate closed her eyes and concentrated.

Think!

And suddenly she was seeing what he was seeing. It was as if she were inside his head, looking through his eyes. She could see the knife that he was holding in his hand, the long, evil blade slicing through the air as he carried it ahead of him. She could see the narrow basement with the cables snaking along the walls. She could see a patch of dark shadow between two of the generators and knew, with sheer terror, that this was where she was hiding and that he was looking straight at her.

But did he know she was there? She could only see the pictures. She couldn't hear any words.

He began to walk towards her and for Kate it was as if she were watching herself on television. There was nothing she could do. She was about to be killed but at the same time she was the killer, watching with his eyes. She couldn't scream. She couldn't run. She could only wait.

He stopped in front of her. But she knew he hadn't seen her because she couldn't see herself. He was hesitating, uncertain. If she was going to do anything, she would have to do it now.

Kate screamed and lashed out with her foot, kicking Mr Spencer with all her strength.

Mr Spencer swung with the knife. And now Kate felt the movement. She felt the signal from the brain to the hand. She knew what he was going to do at the very second he decided to do it.

She dived down. The knife missed her.

And then there was a brilliant flash. A scream. Sparks exploded all around her and the link between her and the French teacher was ripped apart. The knife had gone over Kate's head and into one of the cables behind her. If she had been reading Mr Spencer's mind at that moment, she would have known what it was like to be electrocuted. The teacher was still standing. Electricity crackled and flared. A smell of burning filled the air. Then there was a bang as the generator short-circuited and he toppled to one side.

Sobbing, Kate dragged herself to her feet and, half blind, with smoke in her eyes and the smell in her nostrils and a scream still trapped in her throat, she staggered out of the room.

Her hearing aid had been knocked out of her ear. Automatically, she pressed it back in again. It was silent. She could hear nothing. It was finally over.

X

Nobody ever found out what happened that night.

Heidi was the only person who saw Kate when she staggered out, pale and trembling, from the empty school. Of course she was worried. Kate didn't say a word as the two of them drove home. She sat hunched up in the back seat of the Nissan, her arms crossed and her hands clutching her shoulders. Looking in the driver's mirror, Heidi could see that she was crying. When they got home, the German au pair wanted to call a doctor but she let Kate dissuade her. After all, her English was so poor. And she had already decided to return to Heidelberg. She didn't want any trouble.

Kate dealt with it her own way. She didn't sleep that night, or for many nights to come. But she had decided not to tell anyone about her involvement in Mr Spencer's death. There were too many difficult questions. All her life she had battled against the idea of being thought different. If the truth came out, she knew people would treat her like a freak. She didn't even tell Martin what had happened. When he asked, a few days later, she told him that when he had failed to show up outside the school, she had left too.

Nobody ever found out.

Brierly Hall was closed for three days after Mr Spencer's rigid, blackened body was discovered by the school janitor in the generator room. In that time, Kate was able to recover. And the police were able to begin their investigations – even if this was one mystery they soon decided they were never going to solve.

They must have realised that Mr Spencer had, after all, killed his wife. How else could they explain the fact that the murder weapon had at last been found – still gripped in the dead man's hand? But they never managed to explain what he had been doing in the basement – nor why he had plunged that same knife into the main power cable in what looked like a bizarre form of suicide.

The police examined everything. They asked questions. They examined everything again. And eventually they went away. Nobody at the school ever heard anything more. Presumably the case was shuffled away into some filing cabinet marked: UNSOLVED.

Meanwhile, Mr Spencer was buried at Saint Mary's

Church, Harrow-on-the-Hill. At the last minute, it was decided that the school should send a small deputation. Two teachers and three children would attend the funeral, as a sign of respect. Mr Fellner, the head, asked for volunteers at morning assembly and, to her own surprise, Kate found herself raising her hand. She didn't want to go. She wanted to forget all about him. But at the same time, it seemed somehow right that she should be there. A final curtain. A chance to say goodbye for ever.

And that was how she found herself on a brilliant winter's day, standing in a cemetery with Martin at her side and Mr Fellner wrapped in a thick black coat just behind her. The sun was shining but there was a deep chill in the air and the ground was icy hard. Martin was shivering, stamping his feet and wondering why on earth he was there. There was only a handful of mourners clustered around the open grave. Kate noticed the Detective Inspector among them. The last time she had seen his face it had been on TV.

A bell began to toll and four men in dark suits appeared, walking out of the church with the coffin stretched out on their shoulders. Kate looked away, wishing more than ever that she hadn't come. A rosy-faced vicar led the way, his prayer book clutched against his chest. A blackbird dropped out of the sky and perched on a gravestone as if interested in what was taking place.

The coffin drew closer. Dark brown oak with brass handles.

'Ashes to ashes...' the vicar began.

Kate's hearing aid crackled.

And then the voice.

'I'll come back. I'll get you one day...'

And Kate began to scream.

BURNT

July 10th

Three weeks in Barbados. A smart hotel on the beach. Surfing, sailing and water-skiing. All expenses paid. It sounds like the star prize on a TV game show and I suppose I ought to be over the moon. Or over the Caribbean anyway. But here's the bad news. I'm going with Uncle Nigel and Aunt Sara.

Mum told me this morning. The new baby is due in the middle of August and she's not going anywhere. There's no question of Dad going anywhere without her. He's gone completely baby mad. If he spends any more time in Mothercare they'll probably give him a job there. The point is, if I don't go with Nigel and Sara, I'm not going to get a summer holiday and Mum thinks it would be easier for everyone if I was out of the way. This is what comes of having another baby thirteen years after the last one. The last one, of course, was me.

A NOTE ON SARA HOWARD.

She's quite a bit older than Mum and looks it. Forty-something? She's fighting a battle with old age and I'm afraid she's not on the winning side. Grey hair, glasses, a slightly pinched face. She never smiles very much although Mum says she was a laugh when she was young. She has small, dark eyes that give nothing away. Dad says she's sly. It's certainly true that you can never tell what she's thinking.

She has no children of her own and Mum said she was happy to take me with her to Barbados but I know this is not true. I overheard them talking last night.

SARA: I'm sorry, Susan. I can't take him. The thing is, I have plans.

MUM: But Tim won't get a holiday if you don't help out, Jane. He'll be as good as gold and we'll pay his way…

SARA: It's not a question of money…

MUM: You said you wanted to help.

SARA: I know. But…

And so on. I wondered why she was being so difficult. Maybe she just wanted to be on her own with Uncle Nigel.

A note on Nigel Howard.

I don't like him. That's the truth. First of all, he's such an awkward, ugly man that I feel embarrassed just being with him. He's tall, thin and bald. He has a round, pale face, no chin but a very long neck. He reminds me of a diseased ostrich. All his clothes came from Marks and Spencer and none of them fit. He's the headmaster of a small private school in Wimbledon and he never lets you forget it. All in all, he has the same effect on me as five fingernails scratching down a blackboard. I wonder why Sara married him?

August 12th

Stayed last night in N & S's house in West London. A Victorian terrace with rising damp. Cases packed and in the hall. We're waiting for the taxi that hasn't arrived. My uncle and aunt had quite an argument about it. He blamed her for not calling the firm that he always uses.

NIGEL: Speedway are much more reliable. Why didn't you call Speedway?

SARA: Because you're always telling me they're too expensive.

NIGEL: For God's sake, woman! How much do you think it's going to cost us if we miss the plane?

Then they argued about the packing. It turns out that Uncle Nigel is absolutely determined to get a sun tan. I wouldn't have said this was possible as he has pale, rather clammy skin that looks as if it's never even seen the sun. Dad once told me that his nickname at the school where he teaches is Porridge…which is, I'm afraid, more or less his colour. Anyway, Nigel wanted to be certain that Sara had packed his sun tan oil and in the end she was forced to open the case and show him.

He had six bottles of the stuff! He had those bottles that come locked together with different sun protection factors. The higher the factor number, the greater the protection. He had oil to go on first thing in the morning and more oil for last thing at night. He had water-resistant oil, hypo-allergenic oil and UVA-protective oil. But he still wasn't satisfied. 'Have you opened this?' he asked, taking out one of the bottles. 'Of course I haven't opened it, dear,' Sara said. She put the bottle back in the case and closed it up again.

The taxi has just arrived. Uncle Nigel was so angry about how late it was that he smashed a vase in the hall. It was the vase Mum gave to Aunt Sara for her birthday. She's sweeping up the pieces now.

August 15th
Things are looking up.

Barbados is a really ace place. Palm trees everywhere and sea so blue it's dazzling. When you go swimming you see fishes that come in every shape and colour and the night is filled with steel drums and the smell of rum. The beaches go on for ever and it's boiling hot, at least ninety. Our hotel is on the west of the island, near Sandy Lane Bay. It's small and modern but right on the beach and friendly and there are other boys of my age staying here so I'm not going to be on my own.

Anyway, N & S have more or less forgotten me which suits me fine. Sara has spent the last two days beside the pool, under a big sun umbrella, reading the latest Stephen King. Nigel doesn't like Stephen King. He gave us a long lecture over dinner about how horror stories are unhealthy and pander to peoples' basest instincts…whatever that means. Apparently he banned Goosebumps from his school.

He's bagged a sun lounger out on the beach and he spent the whole day out there, lying on his back in his baggy Marks and Spencer swimming trunks. He made Sara rub Factor 15 all over him and I could tell she didn't much enjoy it. Without his clothes on, Nigel manages to be scrawny and plump at the same time. He has no muscles at all and his little pot belly hangs over the waistband of his trunks. He has a thin coating of ginger hair. I suppose he must have been ginger before he went bald. I watched

Sara sliding her hands over his chest and shoulders, spreading the oil, and I could see the look on her face. It was as if she was trying not to be sick.

While she read and he sunbathed, I went out with Cassian who's thirteen and who's here with his family for two weeks. They come from Crouch End which isn't too far from where I live. We went swimming and snorkelling. Then we played tennis on the hotel court. Cassian's going to ask his mum and dad if we can hire a jet ski tomorrow but he says they'll probably only pay for a pedalo.

Dinner at the hotel. Uncle Nigel complained about the service and Sara asked him to keep his voice down because everyone was listening. I thought they were going to argue again but fortunately he was in a good mood. He was wearing a white polo shirt, showing off his arms. He says that he's got a good foundation for his tan. I've noticed that whenever he passes a mirror he stops and looks at himself in it. He's obviously pleased although if you ask me, he's looking rather red.

He says that tomorrow he's going to move down to Factor 9.

August 16th
Uncle Nigel has burnt himself.

He didn't say as much but it's pretty obvious. We had lunch in a café on the beach and I could see that his skin was an angry red around his neck and in the fleshy part of his legs. He also winced slightly when he sat down, so his back is probably bad too. Sara said she'd go into Bridgetown and buy some calamine lotion for him but he told her that he was perfectly all right and didn't need it.

But he did say he'd move back on to Factor 15.

It's very strange this business of the tan. I don't quite understand what Uncle Nigel is trying to prove. Sara told me (while he was in the toilet) that it's the same every year. Whenever he goes on holiday he smothers himself in oil and lies rigidly out in the open sun but he never has much success. I suppose his obsession must have something to do with his age. A lot of parents are the same. They get into their forties and off they go to the gym three times a week, pushing and pedalling and punishing themselves as they try to put a bit of shape back into their sagging bodies. Uncle Nigel's body is beyond hope as far as muscles are concerned. But at least he can give himself a bit of colour. He wants to go back to school bronzed and healthy. Perhaps for one term they'll stop calling him Porridge.

They didn't let me hire a jet ski even though it's my own money. Mum and Dad gave me a hundred pounds to spend. So Cassian and I went for a walk and then played football with some local kids we met. Before we left, I saw Nigel, stretched out in his usual place. He was reading *A Tale of Two Cities* by Charles Dickens but the oil and sweat were dripping off his fingers and blotching the pages. He also had the sun in his eyes and was having to squint horribly to read the words. But he won't wear sunglasses. He doesn't want them to spoil his tan.

Got back to the hotel at six o'clock. Uncle Nigel was having a shower by the pool. I could see that he'd fallen asleep in the sun. He was very red. At the same time, he must have left the Dickens novel leaning against him when he dropped off because there was a great rectangle on his stomach – the same size as a paperback book – which was as white as ever. The sun lounger had also made a wickerwork pattern on his back.

I waved to him and asked him how he was. He said he had a headache. He also had a heat blister on one cheek.

August 17th

Cassian's parents took me out for the day. We drove in an open-top jeep through the centre of the island. Lots of sugar cane and old plantation houses that make you think of pirates and slaves. We visited a cave. We had to wear plastic hats for protection and a tram took us deep down into the ground, through amazing caverns with petrified waterfalls, stalagmites and stalactites. I can never remember which is which. Cassian's dad is a writer. His mum is some sort of TV producer. The two of them didn't argue, which made a change.

I was sort of dreading getting back to the hotel, wondering about N & S. No surprises there. He was still out on his sun lounger and Sara was sitting next to him, reminding him to turn over every half hour...like a chicken on a spit. She told me that he had decided he would be all right with Factor 9 again but I wouldn't have agreed. His shoulders were badly burned and there were two more blisters on his nose.

She rubbed in some more oil for him. I was surprised how horrible it smelled. It's yellow and it oozes out of the bottle, rippling between her fingers as she rubs it in. Disgusting.

I've caught the sun a bit myself but I'm being careful. I wear a T-shirt with wide sleeves and a Bart Simpson baseball cap. I've got my own sun cream too. If you ask me, Uncle Nigel is out of his mind. Hasn't he heard of skin cancer?

August 19th

He's got a tan! It's not exactly a Mr Universe shade of bronze but he's definitely brown from head to toe. There are one or two areas where the skin is still a bit red, under his arms and on the very top of his head, but he says they'll soon blend in with the rest of him. He was in a really good mood this afternoon and even said that perhaps I can go on a jet ski after all.

It rained for the first time this afternoon. The rain out

here is strange. One moment it's blazing sunlight and the next it's just bucketing down and everyone has to run for cover. But it's not like English rain. The water is softer. It's like standing in a warm shower. And it's over as quickly as it started, as if someone threw a switch.

Sara took me on the bus to Bridgetown, leaving Nigel on the beach (Factor 4). We walked round the port which was a jumble of sailing boats and huge, fat cruisers. She looked into chartering a boat for the day but when she found out the price she soon forgot that idea. Nigel would never agree to pay, she said, and at the same time she sort of sighed. So I asked her something I'd always wondered. 'Why did you marry Uncle Nigel?' I asked. 'Oh,' she said. 'He was very different when he was young. And so was I. I thought we'd be happy together.'

We went to a bar down on the dock. Sara bought me an ice cream. For herself she ordered a large rum punch even though it was only half past three in the afternoon. She made me promise not to tell Uncle Nigel.

August 21st
Bad news. Uncle Nigel has completely peeled. So now he's back to square one.

August 22nd
Uncle Nigel spent the entire day (eight hours) on the

beach but it looks as if his new skin is refusing to tan. He has moved down to sun protection Factor 2.

He and Sara had an unpleasant argument yesterday... the day he lost his tan. Apparently, when they woke up, the sheets were covered with bits of brown. At first Sara thought it was mould or something that had flaked off the ceiling. But it was actually dead skin. She said it made her feel sick and Nigel just flew at her. You could hear their voices down the corridor.

I saw Nigel stripping off on the beach. There was a bright pink strip going from his neck to his belly as if someone had been trying to unwrap him in a hurry. This was where the old skin had fallen away. But new skin had already grown to take its place. As for the rest of his tanned skin, it was obvious that he was going to lose that too. It was already muddy and unhealthy. He couldn't move without a bit flaking off. He was doing what he could to save it. I noticed that he'd brought down a big bottle of After Sun and he was rubbing that in as if he thought it would somehow stick him back together again. I didn't think it would work.

I went out again with Cassian and also with his older brother, Nick. I told them about Uncle Nigel and they both thought it was very funny. Nick told me that in Victorian times nobody wanted to have a sun tan. It was considered socially inferior. This is something he learned at school.

When I got back to the hotel, Uncle Nigel was still lying there with Aunt Sara just a few metres away, sitting with her Stephen King under an umbrella. The book must have been amusing her because there was a definite smile on her face.

As for my uncle, I think the whole situation is getting out of hand. His new skin isn't tanning. But it is burning. It's already gone a virulent shade of crimson. Unlike me, he hasn't been wearing a hat and a large heat bubble has formed in the middle of his head. It's like one of those white blobs you get in cartoons when Jerry hits Tom with a hammer. All the other hotel guests have begun to avoid him. You can see, when they walk down to the sea. They make a circle so they don't have to get too close.

I notice, incidentally, that he's still reading *A Tale of Two Cities*. But we've been here now for almost two weeks and he's still only on page twelve.

August 25th

Cassian and Nick left today and the hotel feels empty without them. Another family arrived...three girls! To be honest, I'm beginning to look forward to going home. No news from Mum. She still hasn't had the baby. I'm missing her. And I'm really worried about Uncle Nigel.

All his old skin has gone now. It's either fallen off or it's been taken over by the new skin which is a sort of mottled mauve and has a life of its own. His whole body is covered in boils like tiny volcanoes. These actually burst in the hot sun…I swear I'm not making it up. They burst and yellow pus oozes out. You can actually see it. Every ten minutes he seems to have another boil somewhere on his skin. There are also lots more sores on his face. They run down the side of his cheeks and onto his neck. If he had a chin I'm sure that would be covered in sores too.

And he's still trying to get a tan! This afternoon I'd had enough. I don't often talk to Uncle Nigel. For some reason I always seem to irritate him. But I did try telling him that he looked, frankly, horrible, and that I was really worried about him. I should have saved my breath! He almost chewed my head off, using the sort of language you wouldn't expect to hear coming from a head teacher. So then I tried to tell Aunt Sara what I thought.

ME: Aunt Sara, aren't you going to do something?
SARA: What do you mean?
ME: Uncle Nigel! He looks awful…
SARA: (*with a sigh*) What can I do, Tim? I'm afraid your uncle has never listened to me. Not ever. And he's been determined to get this tan.
ME: But he's killing himself.
SARA: I think you're exaggerating, dear. He'll be fine.

But he isn't fine. Dinner tonight was the most embarrassing night of my life.

We went to a posh restaurant. It should have been beautiful. The tables were outdoors, spread over two terraces. We sat with paper lanterns hanging over us and the silver waves almost lapping at our feet. Nigel walked very stiffly, like a robot. You could tell that his clothes were rubbing against his damaged skin and to him they must have felt like sandpaper.

He didn't make much sense over dinner. He ranted on about a boy called Charlie Meyer who obviously went to his school and who, equally obviously, was no favourite of his. He was still using a lot of four-letter words and I could see the other diners glancing round. One of the waiters came to see what the matter was and suddenly Uncle Nigel was violently sick! All over himself!

We left at once. Uncle Nigel groaned as we bundled him into a taxi. I could feel his skin under his shirt. It was damp and slimy. Aunt Sara didn't say anything until we got back to the hotel. Then... 'You can order from room service, Tim. And you'll have to put yourself to bed.'

'What about Uncle Nigel?'

'I'll look after him!'

August 27th
Uncle Nigel is no longer able to talk. Even if he could

construct a sentence anyone could understand, he would be unable to say it as he has now managed to burn his lips so badly that they've gone black and shrivelled up. What was left of his hair has fallen out and his new skin has shrunk and torn so that you can actually see areas of his skull. I think he has also gone blind in one eye.

The hotel manager, Mr Jenson, has banned him from the beach as the other guests had finally complained. Mr Jenson had a meeting with my aunt and me. He said that in his opinion my uncle shouldn't be sunbathing any more.

JENSON: Forgive me, Mrs Howard. But I think this is a very unhealthy situation...

SARA: I have tried to stop him, Mr Jenson. This morning I even locked him in the bathroom. But he managed to force the window and climb down the drainpipe.

JENSON: Perhaps we should call for a doctor?

SARA: I'm sure that's not necessary...

She said she'd been trying to stop him but I'm not sure that's true. She was still rubbing oil into him every morning and evening. I'd seen her. But I didn't say anything.

I am beginning to feel very uneasy about all this.

August 28th

Yesterday evening, Uncle Nigel ran away.

He had another argument with Aunt Sara. I heard vague, muffled shouts and then the slamming of the door. When I looked out of the window – the sun was just beginning to set – I saw him race out of the hotel, staggering towards the beach. He could hardly stand up straight. He was wearing shorts and nothing else and he was completely unrecognisable. He had no skin at all. His eyes bulged out of his skull and his lips had shrunk back to reveal not just his teeth but his gums. Every step he took, he moaned. At one point he staggered and fell back against the hotel wall. One of the guests saw him and actually screamed.

This morning he was gone. But he had left a bloody imprint of himself on the wall.

August 30th

I can't help but feel that Aunt Sara is completely different. There has been no news of Uncle Nigel and he hasn't been seen for two days but she hasn't been worried. She has been drinking a lot of rum. Last night she got drunk and ended up dancing with one of the waiters.

I can't wait to get home. I spoke to Mum this morning. It seems I have a baby sister. They're going to call her Lucy.

Mum asked me about the holiday. I told her about the

island and about the family I met but I decided not to say anything about Uncle Nigel.

August 31st
Uncle Nigel is dead!

Some fishermen found him yesterday, lying flat on the beach. At first they thought he must have been eaten up and spat out by sharks. His whole body was a mass of oozing sores, gashes and poisoned flesh. He no longer had any eyes. What had happened was that he had fallen asleep again in the sun. And this time he hadn't woken up.

They were only able to recognise him by his Marks and Spencer shorts.

Aunt Sara didn't even sound surprised when they told her. She just said 'Oh.'

And I thought I saw her smile.

September 2nd
Back in England. Thank goodness.

Mum and Dad were meant to meet me at Heathrow Airport but as it turned out there was one last, nasty surprise waiting for me when we finally landed. It turned out that my new sister, Lucy, had caught some sort of virus. It wasn't anything very serious – just one of the things that newly-born babies often get – but she'd had to go back into hospital for the night and Mum and Dad were with her.

Sara's name was called out over the intercom and we lugged our cases over to the information desk where we were given the news. I'd have to stay at her house – just for the night. Mum and Dad would come and pick me up in the morning.

So it was back to Fulham and the Victorian terrace. I have to say that I walked in with a certain feeling of dread. It was Sara's house now, of course. But it had once been Nigel's and I could still feel him in there. It wasn't just his ghost. In a way it was worse than that. The drab wallpaper and the shelves stuffed with fat, serious books. The old-fashioned furniture, the heavy curtains blotting out the light, the smell of damp. It was as if his spirit was everywhere. He was dead. But while we were in the house, his memory lived on.

Aunt Sara must have felt it too. Before she'd even unpacked, she rang an estate agent and told him that she wanted to put the house on the market immediately. She said she planned to emigrate to Florida.

We had supper together – take-away Chinese – but neither of us ate very much and we hardly talked at all. She wanted to be on her own. I could tell. In a funny way, she seemed almost suspicious of me. I noticed her glancing at me once or twice as if she was worried about something. It was as if she was waiting for me to blame her for Nigel's death. But it hadn't been her fault. She hadn't done anything wrong.

Had she?

I went to bed early that night. In the spare room. But I couldn't sleep.

I found myself thinking about everything that had happened. Over and over again the pieces went through my mind until a picture began to form. I rolled over and tried to think of something else. But I couldn't. Because what I was seeing now, what I should have seen all along, was so horribly obvious.

'*I have plans…*'

That's what Sara had told my mum before we left for the holiday. She hadn't wanted me to come from the very start. It was almost as if she had known what was going to happen and hadn't wanted me to be there, as a witness. She hadn't made Uncle Nigel lie in the sun, but now I thought about it, she had never actually discouraged him either. And his death hadn't upset her at all. She'd been drinking rum and dancing with the waiters before they'd even discovered the corpse.

No! It was crazy! After all, she *had* packed all those bottles, the different sun-tan lotions. She'd even rubbed them in for him. As I lay in the darkness, I remembered the yellow ooze spilling out of the bottle, rippling through her fingers as she massaged his back. Once again I smelled it – thick and greasy – and at the same time I remembered something Nigel had said just after we'd arrived. He'd been examining one of the bottles and he'd said:

'Have you opened this?'

Maybe that was what made me get up. I couldn't sleep anyway so I got up and went downstairs. I don't know why I tiptoed but I did. And there was Aunt Sara, standing in the kitchen, humming to herself.

She was surrounded by bottles. I recognised them at once. Factor 15, Factor 9 and Factor 4. The water-resistant oil, the hypo-allergenic oil and all the other oil. The Before Sun and the After Sun protection. She was emptying them, one at a time, into a large green tin. And no matter what it said on the labels, it was the same gold-coloured oil that poured into the tin and I guessed that this was where the oil had really come from in the first place.

QUIKCOOK VEGETABLE OIL – FOR FASTER FRYING

Big red letters on the side of the tin. My aunt continued emptying the bottles, getting rid of the evidence. I crept back to bed and counted the hours until my parents finally came.

FLIGHT 715

There are some nightmares so horrible that even when you wake up they won't quite go away. You lie in bed with the grey light of the morning beating at the window and even though you're in your own bed, in your own room, you still wonder. Because the creatures of your dreams, the ghosts and the monsters are still with you, hiding in the shadows, just out of sight. And maybe you lie there for five minutes, for ten minutes, thinking about it, wondering. But finally you convince yourself – you have to. It was only a dream.

Judith Fletcher had just such a dream on the last day of her holiday in Canada and even as her parents slept on in their room and her younger sister, Maggie, snored noisily in the bed next to her, she lay there and remembered.

This was her dream.

She was at a funeral. There was something wrong with the cemetery. It was far too big and the grass simply didn't look like grass. It was as flat as cardboard and that strange colour that you only see in dreams; a green-silver-grey that had no name. There was a church bell ringing and, in the distance, a clock showing three minutes past six. Judith didn't walk into the cemetery. She was carried, lifted by unseen hands. It was only as she floated towards a single grave, a black rectangle that seemed to have been cut out rather than dug, that she felt the first wave of terror. This wasn't any funeral. This was hers.

She tried to wake up but sleep had become a prison. She tried to scream but only the faintest whisper escaped her lips.

And then she saw the mourners. There were about three hundred of them, standing round the grave, none of them speaking. Even though she was asleep, it struck her as curious that none of them had dressed for the funeral. They were wearing their everyday clothes, watching her with empty, blank faces. Most of them were carrying suitcases. Some had duty-free bags.

There was a fat woman with big eyes and a shock of curling hair. A little boy holding a teddy bear that was missing an arm. A sullen-faced husband and wife, holding hands, not talking to each other. A black man in a leather jacket, biting his fingernails. Later on, she would remember every one of them as if she had known them all her life, even though she was certain she had never seen them before.

And then there was the vicar. At least, Judith assumed he was the vicar as he seemed to be in charge. But at the same time she was aware that the man wasn't wearing church clothes; indeed, he seemed to be dressed in some sort of uniform. He was a thin man with long, fair hair. His nose had been broken at some time and there was a thin scar running down his cheek. He was standing alone, nearest the grave, and as Judith arrived he said four words.

'Flight Seven One Five.'

The invisible hands lowered Judith into the grave. Darkness rushed in on her. And that was when the nightmare became unbearable, when she struggled with all her being to break free. She couldn't breathe. She had never known such utter blackness. It seemed to be not just outside her but inside too, at the back of her eyes, in her throat, reaching to the pit of her stomach. She was falling into it, endlessly falling. The tiny rectangle of light that had been the entrance to the grave was now a mile away. At the same time she was aware of two distinct sounds; first a huge explosion, then the scream of ambulances that grew louder and louder until she couldn't take any more.

She woke up.

She wasn't dead. She was alive and lying in a rented flat in Vancouver. Her name was Judith Fletcher and she was thirteen years old. Her father, an architect, had been appointed to work on a new hotel complex in the city and he had taken the opportunity to bring the whole family over to travel round Canada. That was where they had been for the past three weeks. And today they were due to fly back to London.

On Flight 715.

Judith got up, went into the bathroom and splashed cold water over her head. She looked into the mirror. Two blue eyes set in a round, freckled face, with fair hair hanging long on each side, looked back. In the bedroom, she heard Maggie wake up and call out for her. That was Maggie through and through. The only time her eight-year-old sister ever stopped talking was when she was asleep. But Judith ignored her. She had to think.

She knew it had just been a dream, a horrible dream. But at the same time she was certain that it was something more. It had all been so real. She had dreamed before, but never in such detail. And no dream had stayed with her the way that this one had. She could still remember everything. And even as the water trickled down her cheeks and dripped off her chin, she realised that this dream had one other difference too. She knew what it meant.

It couldn't have been simpler. She was going to die. At three minutes past six…that was the time she had seen on the clock. She even knew how she was going to die. The vicar-who-wasn't-a-vicar had told her.

Flight 715.

The plane was going to crash.

Judith wasn't superstitious. She didn't believe in ghosts, witches, UFOs, telepathy...or any of the other things that the boys at school were always talking about. She had watched one or two episodes of *The X Files* but the stories hadn't interested her simply because she couldn't take them seriously. Just because something couldn't be explained, that didn't make it supernatural. There was no such thing as the supernatural. That was what she had always thought.

Until now.

Now she remembered – there was a word for what she had experienced. Clairvoyance. There were people who dreamed things that were going to happen, things that did happen. They were called clairvoyants. And they weren't all weirdos either. Judith's history teacher had once said that Joan of Arc was a clairvoyant. So was the American president, Abraham Lincoln, who had actually dreamed of his own assassination a week before it happened! A writer – Mark Twain – had dreamed of the death of his brother. There was even some guy who had described the sinking of the Titanic in every detail...fourteen years before it had happened.

The dream had changed everything. Simply because she knew in her heart that it hadn't simply been a dream. It had been something altogether more frightening. A warning. It didn't matter what she believed or what she didn't believe. She couldn't ignore what she had seen.

She left the bathroom and went back into her bedroom to get dressed. Sweatshirt, jeans, trainers and baseball cap. Her parents were also awake and had quickly fallen into the chaos of last-minute packing.

'Where are the tickets?' she heard her dad call out from the other room.

'By the bed.' That was her mum. Sandra Fletcher worked as a hospital administrator. She had taken unpaid leave in order to make the trip.

And in a few hours time, the four of them would be boarding a plane, Flight 715 to London, and they would all die. At three minutes past six (the plane was due to land at a quarter past six in the morning) something would go horribly wrong and…

'Do you want some breakfast, girls?'

Mark Fletcher had put his head round the door, breaking off Judith's thoughts. He was a fit, athletic man in his early forties, just a few streaks of grey in his hair.

'I'm starving!' Maggie was standing on her bed. Now she began to jump up and down, her pigtails flying. She's excited about the flight, Judith thought.

The flight...

She said nothing while Sandra served up their last Canadian breakfast: waffles and crisped-up bacon with maple syrup. There were cases everywhere. The family had taken so much luggage with them that they had almost been charged extra at Heathrow and since then they'd added several kilograms of souvenirs, clothes and – ever since the girls had found they were half-price in Canada – rollerblades and CDs. Her mother pushed a plate in front of her but she ignored it. She had been frightened by what had happened. But she was almost as frightened at the thought of what she now had to do.

'What's the matter, Judith?' Mark Fletcher had noticed the look on his daughter's face.

'I'm not going home.' And there it was. She'd done it, said it. As easy as that.

Mark laughed. 'Thinking about school, are you?'

'Holidays have to end some time, Judith,' her mother said.

'No.' Judith's face was almost expressionless. 'I'm not going on the plane.'

Her parents exchanged a look, a little puzzled now.

'What do you mean?' her father asked.

'She's scared!' Maggie giggled and dipped her finger into the maple syrup, drawing a circle on her plate.

'The plane's going to crash,' Judith said. 'I'm not going on it. None of us are.'

Sandra had been holding a mug of coffee. She put it down. 'What are you talking about, darling?' she said. She sounded so reasonable but Judith knew she wouldn't be that way for long. 'You've never been scared of flying.'

'I'm not scared. I mean, I'm not scared of flying. But I'm not going on that flight. 715...'

Mark smiled, still trying not to take his daughter too seriously. 'We can't change the tickets,' he said. 'You know that.'

'We can buy new ones.'

'Do you have any idea how much that would cost?'

'There's no question of buying new tickets!' Sandra exclaimed. 'What is all this, Judith? Why are you being so silly?'

'I'm not being silly...' She had to tell them, even though she knew what they would say. 'I had a dream.'

'A dream!' Her mother relaxed. Judith saw she was relieved. A dream was something she could handle. It was something she understood. 'We all have bad dreams,' she said.

'It's only natural.' Mark took over from his wife. 'It's a long flight. Uncomfortable...'

'Airline food!'

'Yuk!' That was Maggie's contribution.

'Nobody enjoys flying,' Mark went on. 'But just because you have a bad dream about something doesn't mean anything's going to happen.'

Judith felt a sudden sadness. She had never known her parents to be so predictable. 'It wasn't an ordinary dream,' she said. 'It was different. I was in a cemetery…'

'We don't really need to hear about it,' Sandra interrupted. She was a little bit angry now and somehow that was predictable too. 'For Heaven's sake! You're thirteen years old now, Judith. You know what dreams are!'

'You'll have forgotten it before we get to the airport,' Mark said.

'I'm not going to the airport.'

Mark and Sandra looked at each other again, suddenly helpless. Judith knew what they must be thinking. She had never behaved this way before. But she had never felt this way either. Even now, sitting with her breakfast in front of her and cases everywhere – everything so normal – she felt as if she were only half there. The other half was still trapped in the dream. And she knew. That was the worst of it. She knew with cold certainty that she was right but that there was nothing she could do or say that would persuade them. Judith had never been more alone.

Her father tried another approach. Humour her. Reason with her. And if that doesn't work get angry with her.

Practical Parenting for Difficult Daughters. Chapter Three.

'This is ridiculous, Judith. Nothing's going to happen to the plane.'

'You're just upsetting Maggie.'

'Anyway, there's no point arguing about it. We're leaving on Flight 715 at midday. If you're really so childish that you're going to let a dream upset you, that's your look out.'

'But what if I'm right, Dad?' Judith knew it was hopeless but she had to try one last time. 'What if it wasn't a dream? What if it was…something more?'

'You don't believe that nonsense. You've never believed it.'

'You've been watching too much television.'

'You know, Judith, this is so stupid…'

And it was that last line, the scorn and the superiority in her father's voice, that resolved her. She had known what she was going to do, almost from the moment she had left the bathroom, but she had been unsure she would have the strength to do it. Now she acted without thinking. Suddenly she stood up. Then, before anyone could stop her, she pushed away from the table, jumped over one of the suitcases and ran out of the room, slamming the door behind her.

'Judith…?' Her father called out. But even if he had guessed what Judith was planning, it was already too late.

Judith ran across the hall, her heart thudding so hard it made her ears ring. Without stopping, she reached the front door. It wasn't locked. Her hand was trembling as she turned the handle and opened it. And then she was out in the warm sunshine, running across the lawn and on to the pavement.

The sidewalk. That's what they call it in Canada.

It was a crazy thought. But it was all crazy. *She* was crazy. That was what her parents would think. Before they murdered her.

She would worry about that later. The apartment was on Robson Street in one of the busiest parts of Vancouver. In less than a minute Judith had been swallowed up by the crowd of morning commuters. Even if her parents had realised what she had done and followed her out they would never find her.

She had been round the city only the day before and knew where she was going. She made her way down to the waterfront and found a snack bar with a view across the lake to the Burrard Inlet with mountains and pine trees behind. She had ten dollars in her pocket. Enough for a few drinks. Enough to allow her to stay as long as she needed.

Judith Fletcher eased herself into a plastic chair, pulled her baseball cap down over her eyes – hiding herself from the world – and prepared to wait until the flight had left.

*

Her parents, of course, were furious when she slunk back to the apartment just before midday. She had never seen them so angry. Their anger almost made them ugly, twisting their faces, burning in their eyes.

'How could you, Judith? We've been looking everywhere for you!'

'We've been worried sick about you. A young girl out in the city on her own!'

'Do you know how much this is going to cost us?'

'Were you out of your mind?'

'When we get back to England, you are going to pay for this, young lady. I don't know how… But you're going to pay!'

Her father had never smacked her. Not once in her entire life. This time, Judith knew he had come close. Perhaps if she had been a boy it would have been easier. A quick whack with a slipper and the tension would have been released. Instead, her parents' anger slowly wore itself out and the rest of the day was spent in a silence as flat and as unforgiving as the cemetery of her dream. Mark Fletcher made a telephone call and managed to persuade the airline to take them – at no extra charge – on a flight the following day. That at least helped. The bags remained packed. Maggie, silent herself for once, read comics and watched TV. Mark worked. Sandra went for a walk, bought a take-away lunch for them all (Judith didn't eat) and killed time.

The afternoon crept slowly on. Maggie watched more television, then went out for a walk with her father. Sandra wrote a letter. Judith spent most of the time sitting by herself. She was ignored by everyone. Her parents were sullen. Maggie seemed completely baffled…as if her big sister had been taken over by someone else.

And all the time Judith thought about Flight 715. Where was it now? Crossing the Arctic Circle? Dipping south over the Atlantic? The strange thing was, even now she had no doubts. The plane was due to land at ten o'clock Canadian time and she still knew with a horrid, cold certainty that at that moment her parents would understand. The plane would crash. The dream had told her as much. She thought of the passengers. All of them would die. She could almost see the fireball of flame, hear the ambulances tearing across the runway as she had heard them that morning in bed. Now she was guilty. Shouldn't she have warned them too? Couldn't she have stopped the plane from taking off? No. She forced the thoughts out of her mind. She couldn't have done more than she had done. The rest was out of her control.

But at ten fifteen her parents would understand. And then they would forgive her. Everything would be all right.

At five past ten her father got up and left the room.

Maggie was already in bed but Mark and Sandra hadn't said a word to their other daughter and she knew that they had allowed her to stay up on purpose, that they wanted her to be with them now. Mark made the call from the hallway. Again, he didn't say what he was doing but Judith knew he was calling England.

She heard her father's voice, a low murmur on the other side of the door. Sandra was reading a paperback novel she had bought for the journey home. She flicked a page. There was a rattle, the sound of the telephone receiver being replaced. Mark Fletcher came back into the room.

He stood in the doorway. Judith waited for him to speak. And at last the words came.

'Flight 715 landed at Heathrow fifteen minutes ago. It was ahead of schedule. Now I'm going to bed.'

Judith never knew.

Nor did her parents.

None of them ever found out.

Because they weren't at Heathrow, they didn't see the passengers come off the plane. There were about three hundred of them. Apart from the Fletchers' own empty seats, it had been a full flight.

The first person off the flight was a fat woman with large eyes and a shock of yellow hair. Then a young boy holding a teddy bear that was missing an arm. His parents were right behind him; a sullen-faced husband and wife, holding hands, not talking to each other. They were followed by a black man in a leather jacket. He was biting his fingernails. And so it went on...

The last person off the plane was the pilot. He was a thin man with long, untidy hair. Years ago he had been injured in a motorbike accident. There was a scar on his cheek and he had broken his nose. As he left the plane, he was looking tired and sick. His face was pale. He had been sweating. His shirt was still damp, sticking to his chest.

There were three officials waiting for him. 'Are you all right?' one of them asked.

The pilot shook his head and said nothing.

But an hour later he told his story. The officials sat opposite him across a long table, taking notes.

'It was the plumbing system,' he said. 'It must have sprung a leak. God knows how many gallons of water there were swilling around down there. And then, of course, with the altitude, it froze. Ice is heavier than water...I don't need to tell you that. And it was heavy! I knew something was wrong...the way the plane was handling. But it was only when the stewardess told me they couldn't flush the toilets in economy...'

He smiled but there was no humour in his face.

'Anyway, by then it was too late. There was nothing

I could do. As you know, I radioed ahead. Got all the emergency vehicles waiting. I could just about fly but I wasn't sure I could land. Not with all that weight. It was a full flight.' The pilot had opened a can of coke. He drank it all in one go. 'To tell you the truth,' he went on, 'if there had been one extra ham sandwich on that plane, I don't think we'd have made it.'

'You were lucky,' one of the officials said.

'You're right. I heard that there was a no-show at the last minute. A family of four and a ton of luggage.'

'Why weren't they on the plane?' the official asked.

The two other officials shook their heads. 'I've no idea,' the pilot said. 'But I'm glad they weren't. Because I'm telling you, I'm not exaggerating. If they'd been on that flight and we'd had that extra weight on board...' He crumpled up the can and looked at it for a moment, lying in the palm of his hand. 'None of us would be here now,' he said. 'They saved us.'

He threw the can into a wastepaper basket and quietly left the room.

HOWARD'S END

Howard Blake didn't even see the bus that ran him over. Nor did he feel it. One minute he was running across Oxford Street with a stack of CDs in his hand and the clang of the alarm bell ringing in his ears and the next... nothing. That was the trouble with shoplifting of course. When you were caught you just had to run and you couldn't stop at the edge of the road for such niceties as looking left and right. You just had to go for it. Howard had gone for it but unfortunately he hadn't made it. The bus had hit him halfway across the road. And here he was. Fifteen years old and already dead.

He opened his eyes.

'Blimey!' he croaked. 'This isn't happening.'

He closed them again, counted to ten, then slowly opened them, one at a time. There could be no doubt about it. Unless this was some sort of hallucination, he was no longer in London. He was…

'Oh blimey!' he whispered again.

He was still wearing the same black leather jacket, T-shirt and jeans but he was sitting on a billowing white substance that looked suspiciously like a cloud. No. He couldn't pretend. It *was* a cloud. The air was warm and smelled of flowers and he could hear music, soft notes being plucked out on the strings of what he knew must be harps. About thirty metres away from him there was a pair of gates, solid gold, encrusted with dazzling white pearls. Light was pouring through the bars, making it hard to see what was on the other side. And there was something strange about the light. Although it looked very much like sunshine, the sky was actually dark. When Howard looked up he could see thousands of stars, set against a backdrop of the deepest, darkest blue. It seemed to be both night and day at the same time.

Howard was not alone. There was a queue stretching back as far as he could see…stretching so far that even the people in the middle were no bigger than pinpricks. Looking at the ones who were closer to him, he saw that there were men and women from just about every country in the world and dressed in an extraordinary variety of clothes from three-piece suits to saris, kimonos and even eskimo furs. A great many of them were old but there were also teenagers and even young children among them. They were waiting quietly, as if they had always expected to end up here and were cheerfully resigned now that they'd arrived.

But arrived where?

The answer, of course, was obvious. Howard had only ever been to church once and that was to steal the silver candlesticks on the altar, but even he got the general idea. The queue, the clouds, the harps, the pearly gates…it took him right back to Cross Street Comprehensive and Religious Education classes with Doris Witherspoon. So the old bat had been right after all! There *was* such a thing as heaven. The thought almost made him giggle. 'Our Father who art in heaven…' How did the rest of the prayer go? He'd forgotten. But the point was, he'd always assumed that heaven and hell were just places they made up to scare you into being good. It was remarkable to discover that it was actually true.

He stood up, his feet sinking gently into the cloud which shifted to take his weight. Howard was not particularly bright. He'd only been to school half a dozen times that year and had fully intended to stop altogether as soon as he turned sixteen, but now his brain began to grind into motion. He was in a queue of people outside the gates of Heaven. All the people were presumably dead. So it had to follow that he must be dead too. But how had it happened? He couldn't remember being murdered or anything like that. Had he been ill? It was true he'd smoked at least ten cigarettes a day for as long as he could remember, and his mother was always warning him he'd get cancer – but surely he'd have noticed if it had actually happened.

He thought back. That morning he'd woken up in his house on the estate where he lived just outside Watford. He'd eaten his breakfast, kicked the dog, sworn at his mother and gone to school. Of course he hadn't actually arrived at the school. He'd missed so many days that the social workers had been round looking for him but as usual he'd given them the slip. He'd gone into town. That's right. Cheated on the tube train, buying a child's fare, then gone to the West End. He'd eaten a second breakfast in a greasy spoon, then gone to a little snooker club behind Goodge Street…the sort of place that didn't ask too many questions when he went in, and certainly not about his age. He'd thought of going to the new James Bond film but he had an hour to kill before it started so he'd decided to do a little shoplifting instead. There were plenty of big stores on Oxford Street. The bigger the store, the easier the snatch. He'd slipped a couple of CDs under his jacket and was just picking out some more when he'd noticed the store detective closing in on him. So he'd run. And…

What had happened? Now that he thought about it, he had seen a blur of red out of the corner of his eye. There'd been a rush of wind and something had nudged his shoulder, very gently. And that was it. That was the last thing he remembered.

However he looked at it, there could only be one answer. He had been killed! No doubt about it! And...

The next thoughts came very quickly, all in a jumble.

Heaven exists. So hell exists. You don't want to go to hell. You want to go to heaven. But there's no way you're going to heaven, mate. Not with your record. Not unless you manage something pretty spectacular. You're going to have to pull the wool over their eyes good and proper and the sooner you get started...

Howard pushed his way into the queue, stepping between a small Chinese man with the ivory hilt of a knife protruding from his chest, and an old woman who was still wearing her hospital identity bracelet.

'What are you doing?' the woman demanded.

'Get lost, grandma,' Howard replied. Even though all the cigarettes had stunted his growth, Howard was still thick-set and muscular. He had a pale face, greasy hair and dark, ugly eyes which – along with his black leather jacket and the silver studs in his ears, left cheek, nose and lip – made him look dangerous. He wasn't the sort of person you argued with, even if you could see that he was no longer alive. True to form the old lady fell silent.

The queue shuffled forward. Now Howard could make

out a figure sitting on a sort of high stool beside the gates. It was an ancient man with long white hair and a tumbling beard. Dress him in red, Howard thought, and you'd have a heavenly version of Father Christmas. But in fact his robes were white. He was holding a large book, a sort of ledger, and there was a bunch of keys tied around his waist. The man turned briefly and Howard was astonished to see two huge wings sprouting out of his back, the brilliant white feathers tapering down behind him. There were two younger men with him and Howard realised with a shiver that he knew who – or at least what – they were. The keepers of the keys. The guardians at the gates of heaven. He threw his mind back, trying desperately to remember what Miss Witherspoon had said. What was the man with the keys called? Bob? Patrick? Percy? No – it was Peter! Saint Peter! That was it! That was the guy he had to persuade to let him in.

It took another hour but at last he reached the gates. By now, Howard had composed himself. He could see heaven in front of him. But he could imagine hell. He knew which he preferred.

'Name?' St Peter (it had to be him) asked.

'Howard,' Howard replied. 'Howard Blake, sir.' He was pleased with the 'sir'. He had to show respect. Butter the old fool up.

'How old are you, Howard?'

'I'm fifteen, sir.' Howard tried to sound very young and innocent. He wished now that he had thought to remove all the silver pins from his face.

One of the younger angels leant forward and whispered to Saint Peter. The old angel nodded. 'You were killed on Oxford Street, this afternoon,' he said.

'Yes, sir. I can't imagine what my old mum will say. It'll break her heart, I'm sure…'

'Why weren't you in school?'

Howard swallowed. If he told them he was playing truant, he'd be done for. He had to think of something. 'Well, sir…' he gurgled. 'It was my mum's birthday. So I asked the teacher if I could take the afternoon to nick something for her…I mean, buy something for her. I wanted to buy her something nice. So I popped into town.'

'Were you always kind to your mother, child?'

Howard remembered all the names he had called her that morning. He thought of the money he had stolen from her handbag. Sometimes he'd stolen the entire handbag too. 'I tried to be a good boy,' he said.

'And did you work hard at school?'

'Oh yes. School is very important. Religious education was always my favourite lesson. And I worked as hard as I could, sir.'

'You look like a strong boy. I hope you never bullied anyone.'

Images flashed in front of Howard's eyes. Glen Roven with a black eye. Robin Addison, crying, with a bleeding nose. Blake Ewing with a twisted arm, shouting while Howard stole his lunch money. 'Oh never, sir,' he replied. 'I hate bullies.'

'Hatred is a sin, child.'

'Is it? Well, I quite like bullies, really. I just don't like what they do!'

Howard was sweating, but the angel seemed content. He made a few notes in his book. He was using a feather pen, Howard noticed. He wondered if the angel had made it out of his own wing.

St Peter peered at him closely and for a moment Howard was forced to look away. The angel's eyes seemed to look right into him and even through him. He wondered how many thousands – how many millions of people those eyes had examined.

'Do you repent your sins?' St Peter asked.

'Sins? I never sinned!' Howard felt his hand curling into a fist and quickly unclenched it. He somehow didn't think it would be a good idea to punch St Peter on the nose. 'Well, maybe I forgot to feed the dog once or twice,' he said. 'And I didn't do my maths homework one evening last June. I repent about that. But that's it, sir. There ain't nothing more.'

There was a soft clunk and Howard noticed that one of

the CDs he had been stealing had fallen out of his leather jacket. He glanced at it, blushing. 'Cor! Look at that!' he said. 'I wonder how that got there?' He picked it up and handed it to St Peter. 'Would you like it, sir? It's Heavy Vomit. They're my favourite group.'

St Peter took the CD, glanced at it briefly, then handed it to one of his aides. He smiled. 'All right, my child,' he said. 'You may go through the gates.'

'I may?' Howard was amazed.

'Enter!'

'Thanks a bunch, sir. God bless you and all the rest of it!'

He had done it! He could hardly believe it. He had smiled and simpered and called St Peter 'sir' and the old geezer had actually bought it. And his reward was going to be heaven! Howard straightened his shoulders. Ahead of him, the gates opened. There was swirl of music as a thousand harps came together in a billowing, flowing crescendo. The music seemed to scoop him up in its arms and carry him forward. At the same time he heard singing, like a heavenly choir. No! It *was* a heavenly choir, ten thousand voices, invisible and eternal, singing out in celestial stereo. The light danced in his eyes, washing through him. He walked on, noticing that his black leather jacket and jeans had fallen away to be replaced by his very own white robe and sandals. He passed through the gates and saw them swing gently shut behind him. There was a click and then it was over. The gates had closed. He was in!

The next few days passed very happily for Howard.

He floated along through a landscape of perfect white clouds where the sun never set, where it never rained and where it was never too hot or too cold. Harp music and the soft chanting of hallelujahs filled the great silence. There wasn't any food or water but that didn't matter because he was never hungry or thirsty. It occurred to him that although there must have been millions and millions of people in heaven, the place was so vast that he didn't see many of them. He did pass a few people who waved at him and smiled pleasantly but he ignored them. He was glad to be there with the other angels but that didn't mean he actually had to talk to them.

It was heaven. Sheer heaven.

The days became weeks and the weeks months. The harps continued to play soft, tinkling music that followed Howard everywhere. The truth was, he was getting a little bit fed up with the harps. Didn't they have drums or electric guitars in heaven? He was also a little sorry that heaven didn't have more colour. White clouds and blue sky were all very well but after a while it was just a bit...repetitive.

He set out now to meet other people deciding that, after all, he would probably enjoy the place more if he wasn't on his own. Certainly the angels were very friendly. Everybody smiled at him. They always seemed happy to see him. But at the same time they didn't have a whole lot to say beyond 'Good morning!' and 'How are you?' and (at least a hundred times a day) 'God bless you!'

Despite the fact that everything was unquestionably perfect, Howard was getting bored and after he had been there for...well, it could have been a year or it could have been ten – it was hard to tell when nothing at all was really happening – he decided that he would purposefully pick a fight, just to see what happened.

He waited until he had found an angel smaller than himself (old habits die hard) and stumped over to him.

'You're very ugly!' he exclaimed.

'I'm sorry?' The angel had been sitting on a cloud doing nothing in particular. But then, of course, there was nothing particular to do.

'Your face makes me sick,' Howard said.

'I do apologise,' the angel replied. 'I'll leave at once.'

'Are you chicken?' Howard cried.

'Am I a chicken?'

'You're scared!'

'Yes. You're absolutely right.'

The angel tried to leave and that was when Howard hit him, once, hard. The angel jerked back, surprised. Howard's fist had caught him square on the chin but there was no blood, no bruising. There wasn't even any pain. It took the angel a moment or two to realise what had happened. Then he gazed sadly at Howard. 'I forgive you,' he said.

'I don't want to be forgiven!' Howard exclaimed. 'I want to have a fight.'

'God bless you!' the angel said, and drifted away.

Another thousand years passed.

The harps were still playing. The clouds were still a perfect, whiter-than-white white. The sky was still blue. The weather hadn't changed, not even a little drizzle for just a minute or two. The choirs sang and the angels wandered along, smiling dreamily and blessing one another.

Howard was tearing his hair out. He had torn it out several times, in fact, but it always grew again. He kicked at a cloud and bit his lip as his foot passed right through it. He hadn't been ill, not once in all the time he had been here. He would have quite liked it really. A cough or a cold. Even a bout of malaria. Anything for a change. Nor had he found anyone to talk to. The other angels were all so...boring! Recently – about a hundred and twenty years ago – he had started talking to himself but he had already discovered that he also bored himself – and anyway he hated the sound of his own voice. He had been in a few more fights but they had all ended as disappointingly as the first and he had finally decided there was no point.

And then, quite by chance one day (he had no idea which day and as there was no night he wasn't even sure if it *was* a day) he realised that he had somehow made his way back to where it had all begun. There were the pearly gates, and standing with his two helpers, there was St Peter, still dealing with the queue that stretched to the horizon and beyond. With the first spurt of hope and excitement he had felt in centuries, Howard hurried forward, the sandals flapping on his feet, his white robes billowing around him.

'Excuse me!' he cried, interrupting St Peter as he talked to a man with a kilt but no legs. 'Excuse me, sir!'

'Yes?' St Peter turned to him and smiled through the bars of the gate.

'You probably don't remember me. But my name is Howard... Howard um...' Howard realised that he had forgotten his own surname. 'I came here quite a long time ago.'

'I remember perfectly well,' St Peter said.

'Well. I have to tell you something!' Suddenly Howard was angry. He'd had enough. More than enough. 'Everything I said when I came here was a lie. I didn't go to school and when I did go to school I bullied everyone, including the teachers. I kicked the cat – or maybe it was a dog. I hated my mum and she hated me. I lied and I cheated and I stole and I know I said I was sorry for what

I'd done but I was lying then too because I'm not. I'm glad I did it. I enjoyed doing it.'

'What are you trying to say?' St Peter asked.

'What I'm saying, you horrible old man, is that I don't like it here!' Howard was almost shouting now. 'In fact I hate it here and I've decided I don't want to stay!'

'I'm afraid you have no choice,' St Peter replied. 'That decision is no longer yours.'

'But you don't understand, you bearded twit!' Howard took a deep breath. 'I'm all wrong for heaven. I shouldn't be in heaven. You should never have let me in.'

The angel didn't speak. Howard stared at him. His face had changed. The beard had slipped, like something you buy at a novelty store. Underneath, the chin was pointed and seemed to be covered in what looked suspiciously like scales. And now that he looked more closely, Howard noticed that there was something poking through the old man's hair. Horns?

'Wait...' he began.

St Peter – or whoever, whatever he really was – began to laugh. Two red flames flickered in his eyes and his lips had drawn back to reveal teeth that were viciously sharp.

'My dear Howard,' he said. 'What on earth made you think you'd gone to heaven?'

THE LIFT

'Let's go over this again,' the Detective Chief Inspector said.

Charles Falcon was a small, unhappy-looking man with greying hair and tired blue eyes. He was wearing a dark suit with a striped tie hanging halfway down his chest. His clothes were, like him, crumpled. He had been a policeman for thirty years and as far as he was concerned that was about twenty years too long. He had lost count of the number of murders he had investigated. The stabbings and shootings, the batterings and stranglings. And that was in addition to the armed robberies, burglaries, kidnappings, and assaults. He was glad it was almost over. Two more months. Then retirement back to Norfolk. A little house in Hunstanton, a dog, long walks along the beach and no more death.

Two more months and then this had to come along.

He was sitting at his desk in New Scotland Yard. There was a second man opposite him, thirty years his junior, neat and enthusiastic. His name was Jack Beagle, and he was a Detective Superintendent. He had his notebook open in front of him.

'Where do you want to start?' Beagle asked.

'From the top,' Falcon said. 'Let's start with the family.'

Beagle flipped through the pages in his book. 'All right,' he said. 'Arthur and Mary Smith live in Steyning. It's a small village near the South Downs. They own the fruit shop there. They have one son, Eric, aged eleven. As a Christmas present, they decided to bring him to London. Christmas shopping, lunch at a pizza restaurant, then the afternoon performance of *The Phantom of the Opera*. They had seats in the circle. A23 to...'

'All right! Get on with it!' Falcon interrupted. That was the trouble with Beagle. Too many details. Give him half a chance and he'd be describing what sort of ice creams they'd had in the interval.

Beagle flicked a page. 'After the show, they went to Covent Garden. There's a place in the new piazza that sells gadgets. Eric wanted a South Park clock. Insisted on it. So although they were tired, they went. They got to the station at a quarter to five. That was when he vanished.'

'Eric Smith,' Falcon muttered. He closed his eyes and sighed.

Covent Garden is one of London's oldest and deepest tube stations. There are only two platforms – the Piccadilly Line runs east and west. There are also no escalators. Four lifts connect the top and the bottom. There's a steep, twisting staircase but not many people use it as it has one hundred and ninety-nine steps.

'It was very busy,' Beagle went on. 'After all, it was only three weeks to Christmas and the station was full of people shopping and all the rest of it. There was quite a crowd waiting for the lift and that was when it happened. This boy, Eric... I'm afraid he doesn't sound a very nice piece of work. A bit spoiled and disobedient...'

'You're not saying his parents did him in?' Falcon cut in, gloomily. He'd investigated just such a case about ten years before.

'Oh no, sir. He's their only son and they dote on him. That's why I mentioned the seats. They were the most expensive in the theatre.'

'Go on.'

'They were waiting for the lifts and there were people all around them. Hundreds of people. The Smiths were at the back of the line. And then what happened was, two lifts arrived at exactly the same time, one next to the other. The queue moved forward and Arthur, Mary and young Eric just managed to squeeze into the lift on the left. But then, for some reason, Eric decided he'd get into the lift on the right. He dodged out of one and into the other. His parents called out to him, but it was already too late. The lift doors closed. Both at the same time. And that was that.'

'So he was in one lift and they were in the other.'

'Yes, sir. They weren't very happy about it. They'd told Eric to stay close to them but, like I say, he doesn't sound like the sort of boy who does what he's told. Even so, they weren't particularly worried. After all, it only takes about a minute to get to the top and both lifts would arrive at exactly the same time.'

'Which they did.'

'Yes, sir. They arrived at the top and the doors opened at exactly the same second. The crowd poured out. And here's the rub! There was no sign of Eric. The boy had disappeared.'

'They were certain he got into the lift.'

'We have a witness – a Mrs Nerricott – who saw him run out of one lift and into the other.'

'Did Mrs Nerricott get into the lift with him?'

'No, sir. There wasn't room. But she definitely saw the door close with the boy inside.'

'All right.' Falcon reached into his pocket and took out a chocolate Rolo. It was his last one. He ate it himself. 'So Eric was in one lift and his parents were in another. Could he have slipped out ahead of them at the top?'

'No. They'd have seen. And anyway, there's the security footage.'

'Let's take another look at it!'

There were closed-circuit television cameras at Covent Garden, just as there are at every London station. The time-coded tape had been sent over to New Scotland Yard and for the tenth time Falcon ran it on his monitor. The film was black and white, a little muddy, but still clear enough. He could see everything.

There were Arthur and Mary Smith, both of them weighed down with a load of bags and packages. Arthur was short and bald, in his late forties. Mary was a slightly mousy woman with permed hair, wearing a thick coat. Eric was standing next to them. He wasn't holding anything. He was plump with jug ears and freckles. His hair was spiky and (Falcon knew from colour photographs sent to his office) ginger. He was wearing combat trousers and a fleece with a scarf around his neck but no jacket.

The film showed exactly what happened. That was the hell of it. The whole thing had been recorded.

At 16:44:05, the two lifts arrived simultaneously at the bottom. The crowd surged forward. Falcon saw Arthur and Mary Smith get into the lift on the left with their son. And there, on the screen, was Eric, suddenly running into the lift on the right, squeezing in behind the crowd. He saw Arthur turn and realise what the boy had done. He saw

Arthur call out although of course there was no sound. Both lift doors were already closing. It was all exactly as Beagle had described.

Cut now to the top floor. There was no camera inside the lifts.

The time on the tape was 16:45:03. Fifty-eight seconds had passed. Both lift doors opened. The lifts at Covent Garden actually have two sets of doors – one at the front and one at the back. You enter the lift from one side but you exit through the other. Arthur and Mary were the last to come out. There were people everywhere, bustling forward through the automatic ticket barriers. The camera mounted over the exit picked up every one of them and Falcon leant forward, examining the faces carefully.

There were old people and young people. Smart people and scruffy ones. A big man with a beard and a wart on his nose fed his ticket into the machine. A teenager carrying a football followed right behind him. Then there was a woman chewing gum, another woman walking with her arms crossed. There was a man blowing his nose into a handkerchief, a second man already lighting a cigar. A Chinese woman with a swollen cheek and an old lady bent over double, supporting herself on a thick walking stick. A constant stream of humanity flowing out of the lift and away from the station.

But there was no sign of Eric. It was an impossible magic

trick. Arthur and Mary were there, on the screen, searching everywhere, beginning to panic. A few minutes later they would call the police. But it was already too late. The boy had gone.

Falcon flicked a button and the picture froze. 'So what do you think?' he asked.

'I don't know, sir.' Falcon had never heard his junior officer sound so defeated. 'I just can't work it out at all. I mean, we can actually see it. That's what beats me. It happened exactly how Mr and Mrs Smith described it!'

'Where are the parents?'

'They're waiting downstairs.'

Arthur and Mary were sitting in a room that smelled of new paint and old disinfectant. Her eyes were red from crying. Her husband had one hand resting on her arm, trying to comfort her, but he looked as lost as she did.

'We don't often come up to London,' he said. 'But Eric insisted. He wanted to go to Hamleys and see this musical.'

'We should have run after him,' Mary stammered. Fresh tears brimmed at her eyes. 'But it was very difficult.'

'We had all his presents,' Arthur explained. 'Eric had chosen a new train set, and the walkie-talkies, the keyboard…'

'…the rollerblades…'

'...and the modelling kit. We had so many bags we could hardly move.'

'My little angel!' Mary wailed.

'He wasn't a complete angel,' Arthur said, gently. 'I mean, we'd told him to stay close to us but he wouldn't listen. And the truth is, he'd been in a bad mood all day. He was very upset when we wouldn't buy him that remote-control helicopter.'

'But it was two hundred pounds!'

'He was also sick after that third ice cream at the theatre. Maybe that was why he decided to run out of the lift like that.' Arthur Smith shook his head. 'We did tell him to stay close.'

'Just find him for us,' Mary said. She took out a handkerchief and dabbed at her eyes. 'He's got to be somewhere!'

Late that night, the two detectives returned to Covent Garden tube station. The tube had already closed down but the station was busy. There were police officers everywhere, searching through the ticket office and moving slowly, step by step, up and down the stairs. There were more policemen below, some with dogs sniffing along the platforms and even following the tracks into the tunnel itself. Both the lifts were being examined by forensic scientists in white coats and plastic gloves. The ticket machine had been opened and all the tickets –

thousands of them – retrieved. There was just a chance that the police might find a fingerprint on one of them. Maybe it would lead them to a maniac, a murderer... but even that wouldn't explain how the eleven-year-old boy with at least thirty complete strangers packed in tight all around him had managed to evaporate into thin air.

Falcon peered into the lift that had carried Eric up. It was an ugly metal box with a heavy sliding door at each end. There was a small window in the side but the glass was too dirty to see through and anyway it was impossible to climb out. There was something almost Victorian about it all. The whole station was grimy and old-fashioned. The passageways, lined with off-white tiles, curved into the distance. The floor was black concrete. With no trains coming and no passengers to add colour and movement, the place was somehow eerie and unnerving. The cold night air whispered over Falcon's neck and he shivered.

He turned to Beagle. 'Have you spoken to anyone who got into the lift with the boy?' he asked.

'No, sir.' Beagle shook his head. 'By the time the parents realised the boy had gone, it was too late. They'd all passed through the ticket barriers and out into the street. We've put up a sign outside asking for people to come forward...'

'Yes. I saw it.'

'…but so far, no luck.'

There was a movement behind them and one of the forensic men appeared clutching a plastic evidence-bag. There were three dirty swabs inside. 'Excuse me, sir…' he began.

'Yes?'

'We've found traces of blood on the floor of the lift.' He handed Falcon the bag. 'Type O. And it's fresh.'

'The boy's?'

'Impossible to say at this stage, sir. But I'd think it's likely.'

'And that's all?'

'One button. Off a shirt. Could be his, could be anyone's. We're going to try and match it up.'

'Thank you…'

Falcon took the lift back up to the surface. He felt almost suffocated, standing inside the metal box. There was a lurch as the lift began to rise and then nothing but the creak of the ancient cables pulling him slowly up. What had happened to Eric Smith when he had taken the lift at a quarter to five that afternoon? He couldn't have climbed on to the roof or anything like that. He couldn't have left it at all until the doors opened. But he had definitely got in and he definitely hadn't got out.

It was enough to drive a detective crazy!

There was a team of policemen on the top floor, examining a great pile of tickets taken out of the machines.

One of them looked up as Falcon emerged from the lift. What was his name? Williams or Willard or something...

'What have you got?' Falcon demanded.

'Nothing very much, sir. Except one thing...'

'Go on.'

'When the used tickets are sucked into the machine, they fall into a compartment, sir. They're emptied regularly throughout the day, but nobody touched the machines after the boy disappeared so at least we've been able to work out more or less where people were coming from at around about a quarter to five this afternoon.'

'And...?'

'Well, it's quite strange really. There were about forty tickets from the same station...Burnt Oak. It struck me as odd...'

'Why?'

'Well, sir. Burnt Oak isn't a very important station, tucked away almost at the end of the Northern Line. And it just seemed strange that so many people should have made the same journey – Burnt Oak to Covent Garden – at exactly the same time.'

'All right, Williams,' Falcon said. 'Have the tickets sent to my office.'

'Yes, sir.' The policeman scowled. 'My name's Willard, sir...'

Later that night, Falcon lay in bed in the small flat he

rented in a back street in Victoria. He was only half asleep. He was trying to dream about Norfolk. He could just picture himself out on the beach, watching the sunset with his dog. What sort of dog would he buy? An Alsatian perhaps? No – that would remind him too much of the police.

But try as he might, he couldn't dream what he wanted to dream. The scene kept changing. There was Eric Smith, standing on the sand in his combat trousers, surrounded by people carrying parcels and shopping bags. Something rose out of the sea. It was the lift. The doors slid open and Eric walked into it. But now the lift had changed. It had become some sort of metallic monster and the doors had been replaced by jagged teeth that sliced down. Eric screamed. The waves rolled in. And Falcon woke up with a start, surprised and relieved to see that it was seven o'clock, the start of another day.

Beagle was waiting for him at the office. 'We've had a breakthrough,' he said.

'Oh yes?' Falcon had bought himself a bacon roll on the way in. It was still in the bag, beginning to get cold.

'One of the men on the screen,' Beagle said. He was pleased with himself and Falcon guessed that he had probably been working all night. 'One of the men in the lift with the boy. I thought I knew him from somewhere and I was right.'

He took out a photograph and slid it on to the desk in front of Falcon. A big man with a beard and a wart on his nose. Falcon remembered him from the security pictures. 'Who is he?' he asked.

'He's a professor at the University of London. Also a writer. His name is Abraham Orlov.'

'Doesn't sound English!'

'I believe he was born in the Ukraine.'

Falcon studied the photograph. 'You said you knew him,' he muttered. 'Has he got a criminal record?'

'No, sir. But I was at London University and although I never met him personally, he stuck in my mind. Do you remember that plane crash about eight years ago?'

Falcon shook his head.

'A small plane went down in the Arctic Circle. There were seventy people on board – mainly academics, geologists…that sort of thing. They'd been studying the ozone layer up in Greenland. It was assumed that they were all killed but in fact more than half of them survived. Stuck in the ice for almost five months.'

'Yes…' Falcon did remember something now. The story had made every newspaper at the time. There was something about it that made him feel uneasy. What was it?

'Orlov was one of them,' Beagle went on. 'He wrote a book about it afterwards. *The Will to Survive*. That was the title. I never read it myself. Anyway, at least it means we've found one person who was in the lift with Eric Smith. I thought you might want to speak to him.'

'Do you have an address?'

Half an hour later, Falcon and Beagle were sitting in a small room in Gower Street, close to the Tottenham Court Road tube station. The room was so cluttered with books that it was almost impossible to move. There were books on shelves, on every seat and in great stacks on the carpet. A pair of tattered curtains hung over a window that looked out on to a bare brick wall. Very little light found its way into the room.

Abraham Orlov was a big man; bigger even than the camera had made him appear. He was wearing a red waistcoat, stretched over a great barrel of a chest and his shoulders were so broad that his head seemed almost lost, balanced on a sprawling cushion of a beard that totally concealed his neck. His hands and wrists were also hairy and he had thick, bushy eyebrows. He wore thin gold spectacles and smoked a pipe that had filled the room with a cloud of blue-grey smoke.

'Yes, indeed, Detective Chief Inspector,' he was saying. He had a loud, hollow voice and an Eastern European accent. 'I was most certainly in London last night.'

'May I ask what you were doing?' Falcon said.

'My dear sir! You may ask what you like! I have

nothing to hide!' He smiled and Falcon felt a shiver of disgust. The man had repulsive teeth. They were yellow and uneven and somehow looked too sharp for a human being. He had seen more attractive teeth than that in a dog. 'Last night was an important anniversary. I met some very dear friends at our club and then we travelled into town together to see a concert.'

'It was your birthday, sir?'

'No, no. You haven't read my book, Detective Chief Inspector?' The eyes twinkled behind the glasses. 'It was exactly eight years since my rescue – our rescue – from the Arctic ice cap. Everyone thought we were dead but then they found we were living. You can imagine, my dear sir, that we survivors became very close, trapped in the wreckage of our plane for so many months. When we were returned to civilisation, we decided to form a club. We purchased our own small club-house, tucked away in the north of this delightful city. Nothing elaborate! It's just somewhere private where we can talk in comfort. And we often meet there…socially.'

'This club house wouldn't happen to be in Burnt Oak, would it, sir?' Beagle asked.

'As a matter of fact it is! Just off the Edgware Road. We all met there at about three o'clock in the afternoon and then travelled into town together.'

'How many of you were there?'

'There are fifty-one members in the club including myself. Not everyone could make it last night but thirty-five of us set out together. On the Northern Line from Burnt Oak station.' He nodded at Beagle. 'Change at King's Cross…'

'Fifty-one members,' Falcon said. He remembered what Beagle had told him that morning. 'But I understood there were seventy people on the plane.'

'Alas, nineteen of them failed to survive,' Orlov said. He twisted his face into an expression of pain. 'You must know the story, Detective Chief Inspector. I made no secret of it. In fact I wrote a book about it. Nineteen people were killed in the crash. The rest of us were trapped. We had water…we could use melted ice. But we had no food. I'm afraid that the will to survive forced us to make a painful decision.'

'Yes, sir?' Falcon said, but he already knew what was coming. Now he remembered the newspaper reports from eight years before.

'We were forced to cannibalise the corpses. For five months we ate nothing but human flesh.' For a brief moment Orlov's tongue appeared, protruding out of his lips above his beard. Then it was sucked back into his mouth. 'It was painful and, of course, disgusting. To cut strips of flesh and lay them out on the wreckage of the aircraft's wings…to dry in the sun. To be forced, day after day, to swallow our unfortunate companions. I don't need to describe it to you. If you want to know more, you should read my book. But it was a simple choice. We could eat or we could die. We chose to live.'

'If I may get back to what happened yesterday,' Falcon said. Suddenly he wanted to get out of this office, away from the smoke, out into the winter sunlight. 'I wonder if you noticed an eleven-year-old boy get into the lift with you at Covent Garden station?'

'I did indeed, Detective Chief Inspector. A rather fat little boy with ginger hair. Wearing baggy trousers and a scarf…'

'That was him.'

'He pushed his way in just before the lift doors closed. Then he forced his way to the front of the lift. He was the first to leave. I was a little worried about him as he seemed too young to be out on his own. But before I could do anything, he was out of my sight. I saw him go through the ticket machine and into the street. But then he was gone.'

'You saw him exit onto the street?' Beagle asked.

'Absolutely.'

'But forgive me, sir.' Beagle was confused. 'The security cameras at the station show you leaving the lift. But there was no sign of the boy.'

Orlov frowned and sucked his pipe. Smoke trickled over his lips and into his beard. 'Could it be, perhaps, that the camera was malfunctioning?' he said at last. 'Because, I assure you, I saw him leave. With my own eyes.'

'It is possible,' Falcon agreed. He stood up. 'Thank you very much, Mr Orlov. I'm sorry to have taken up your time.'

'Anything I can do to help!' Orlov waved a pudgy hand like a king dismissing a courtier.

Falcon paused at the door. 'One last question, sir? Did you go to the concert? You and your friends?'

'Indeed so. Mozart and Brahms. At St Christopher's Church in Covent Garden. It was a delightful evening.'

'And I suppose you went on to dinner afterwards.'

Orlov hesitated, the pipe halfway to his lips. 'No. As a matter of fact we didn't. We weren't hungry.'

The two policemen left.

Falcon said nothing until they got back to New Scotland Yard. Sitting next to him in the car, Beagle had become more and more frustrated and when they reached the office he finally broke out. 'He was lying! That boy never left the lift. And the camera's fine. It's already been checked.'

'I know, Jack,' Falcon said.

The video recorder with the security tape was still there and he turned it back on, but he knew what to expect. He was feeling sick. Just two months until he retired, nine months until he left London for ever. And this had to come along.

Eric Smith had come to London with his parents and just for a laugh he had disobeyed them and slipped into a lift on his own at Covent Garden tube station. Normally nothing would have happened. Normally he would have found himself surrounded by strangers and he would have arrived at the top at the same time as his mum and dad. They would have told him off and he would have sulked and that would have been the end of it. But this hadn't been a normal day. This had been a one in a million chance.

Eric had gone into a lift with thirty-one cannibals, going out for their anniversary dinner. When the doors had closed, he had found himself alone with them for fifty-eight seconds.

Orlov had been lying, of course. He had said that his experience in the Arctic Circle had been painful and disgusting. But Falcon had seen the truth. He had seen it in the flash in those eyes behind the gold-framed spectacles and that little tongue, so pink and moist as it passed over his lips. Perhaps they'd hated it at first, the survivors in that plane. Having to survive for five months, eating human flesh.

But suppose they had come to enjoy it? Suppose they had come to like the taste? They had nineteen bodies. Thirty-eight roast shoulders. Thirty-eight roast legs. One hundred and ninety stewed knuckles. Day after day, they would have sat there, feasting.

But then, after they were rescued, how would they have coped? No more human flesh! Oh yes, they could meet in their little club house and talk about it, relive all those happy meals. But they could only dream of the succulent, pink meat. And all the time they would be hungry, so hungry…

…until a small, plump boy walked right into the middle of them and a door closed and they suddenly realised they couldn't resist it any more and as one they had fallen on him with teeth and nails…

Falcon didn't like to think about it. At least it would have been over for Eric very quickly.

He forced himself to look at the screen. There was Orlov, walking out of the lift. Orlov and his friends. Was it really gum that the woman was chewing? Was the man with the handkerchief blowing his nose or wiping his mouth? That Chinese woman! Was her cheek swollen or was it just that her mouth was full? The old woman with the walking stick! Looking more closely, Falcon could see that the handle was shaped very much like a child's foot. And as for the teenager with the football, he wondered now if it actually was a football at all…

He turned off the machine.

'Are you all right, sir?' Beagle asked.

'No.' Falcon sat staring at the blank screen. Two

questions were going through his mind. How was he going to tell the parents what he knew? And (no wonder Orlov had been so calm) how was he ever going to prove it?

THE PHONE GOES DEAD

This is how Linda James dies.

She's walking across Hyde Park in the middle of London when she notices that the weather has changed. The sky is an ugly colour. Not the blackness of nightfall but the heavy, pulsating mauve of an approaching storm. The clouds are boiling and seconds later there is a brilliant flash as a fork of lightning shimmers the entire length of the Thames.

It has been said that there are two things that you shouldn't do in a storm. The first is to make a telephone call. The second is to take shelter under a tree. Linda James does both of these things. As the rain begins to fall, she runs under the outstretched branches of a huge oak tree, then fishes in her handbag and takes out a mobile telephone.

She dials a number.

'Steve,' she says. 'I'm in Hyde Park.'

That's all she says. There's another flash of lightning and this time Linda is hit full on. Seventy-five thousand volts of electricity zap through her, transmitted through the mobile phone into her brain. Her body jerks and the phone is thrown about twenty metres away from her. This is the last physical action Linda James ever makes and, it goes without saying, she is dead before the telephone even hits the ground.

We will never find out anything more about Linda. Was she married or single? Why was she crossing Hyde Park at six o'clock on a Wednesday evening and does it matter that, wherever she was going, she never arrived? Who was Steve? Did he ever find out that Linda was actually killed at the very moment she was speaking to him? None of these questions will ever be answered.

But the mobile phone. That's another story.

The phone is a Zodiac 555. Already old-fashioned. Manufactured somewhere in Eastern Europe. It is found in the long grass the day after the body has been removed and by a long, circuitous route, it ends up in a second-hand shop somewhere near the coast in the south of England. Despite everything, the phone seems to be working. Linda's SIM-card – the little piece of circuitry that makes it work – is removed. The phone is reprogrammed and another SIM-card put inside. Eventually, it goes back on sale.

And a few weeks later, a man called Mark Adams goes in and buys it. He wants a mobile telephone for his son.

David Adams holds the mobile telephone. 'Thanks, Dad,' he says. But he's not sure about it. A lot of his friends have got mobile phones, it's true. Half of them don't even make any calls. They just think it's cool, having their own phone – and the smaller and more expensive the model, the smarter they think they are. But the Zodiac 555 is clunky and out of date. It's grey. You can't snap on one of those multicoloured fronts. And Zodiac? It's not one of the trendier brand names. David has never heard of it.

And then there's the question of why his father has bought it in the first place. David is sixteen now and he's beginning to spend more time away from home, over-nighting with friends, parties on Saturday evening, surfing at first light on Sunday. He lives in Ventnor, a run-down seaside town on the Isle of Wight. He's lived his whole life on the island and maybe that's why he feels cramped, why he wants his own space. He's talking about sixth-form college and university on the mainland. Mark and Jane Adams run a hotel. They only have one son and they're afraid of losing him. They want to keep him near them, even when they can't see him. And that's why they've bought the mobile phone. David can imagine the next Saturday evening, when he's out with his mates at The

Spyglass, the trill of Bach's Toccata and Fugue (which is what the phone plays when it rings) in his back pocket and his father or his mother checking up on him. 'You're only drinking lemonade, aren't you, David? You won't be home too late?'

But even so, it's his own phone. He can always turn it off. And now that he's started going out with Jill Hughes, who lives in the neighbouring village of Bonchurch and who goes to the same school as him, it could be useful.

Which is why he says, 'Thanks, Dad.'

'That's OK, David. But just remember. I'll pay the line rental for you, but the calls are down to you. It's ten pence a minute off-peak, so just be careful you don't talk too much.'

'Sure.'

They're a close family. For half the year there are just the three of them shuffling about in the twenty-three rooms of The Priory Hotel which stands on a hill, overlooking the beach at Ventnor. Mark and Jane Adams bought it ten years ago, when David was six. They got fed up with London and one day they just moved. Perhaps it was a mistake. The summer season on the Isle of Wight is a short one these days. Package holidays are so cheap that most families can afford to go to France or Spain where they're more sure of good weather. It gets busy around June but this is only March and the place is quiet. As usual it's hard to make ends meet. David helps his dad with the decorating and small maintenance jobs. Jane Adams has a part-time job with a yachting club in Cowes. The three of them get along. Mark still says he prefers Ventnor to London.

David isn't so sure. There are too many old people on the Isle of Wight. Everything feels run-down and neglected. People say that the whole place is fifty years behind the rest of England and he can believe it. Sometimes he looks at the waves, rolling into the shore, and he dreams of other countries – even other worlds – and wishes that his life could change.

It's about to.

The mobile phone rings at half past four one afternoon when David is on his way home from school. Bach's great organ piece reduced to a series of irritating electronic bleeps. Only about six people have his number. Jill, of course. His parents. A few other friends at school. But when David manages to find the phone in his backpack, dig it out and press the button, it is none of them on the line.

'Hello?' It's an old man.

'Yes?' David is sure that it's a wrong number.

'I want you to do something for me.' The old man has one of those slightly quavering, do-what-you're-told voices. 'I want you to go and see my wife at Number Seventeen, Primrose Hill.'

'I'm sorry...' David begins.

'I want you to tell her that the ring is under the fridge. She'll understand.'

'Who is this speaking?' David asks.

'This is Eric. You know my wife. Mary Saunders. She lives at Number Seventeen and I want you to tell her...'

'I know,' David interrupts. 'Why can't you tell her?'

'I can't reach her!' The old man sounds annoyed now. As if he's stating the obvious. 'Will you tell her it's under the fridge? It's under the fridge. She'll understand what you mean.'

'Well...'

'Thank you very much.'

The phone goes dead. David hasn't even asked how Eric Saunders got his telephone number or why he should have rung it to ask him (why him?) to do this favour. But the fact is that David does vaguely know Mary Saunders. Ventnor being the sort of place it is, everyone more or less knows everyone but there's more to it than that. Mary Saunders used to work at the hotel. She worked in the kitchen but she retired about a year ago to look after her husband who had cancer or something. David remembers her; a small, plump, busy woman with a loud laugh. Always cheerful – at least, until she heard the news about her husband's illness. She used to bake cakes and she'd always be there with a cup of tea and a slice of something when David got back from school. She was all right. And Primrose Hill is only a few minutes' walk from where David is now, from where he took the call.

It's strange, Eric calling him this way, but David decides that after all it's not too much to ask. He hasn't even stopped walking. His footsteps carry him to Primrose Hill.

Number Seventeen is part of a long terrace of almost identical houses, tall and narrow, standing shoulder to shoulder on a steeply rising lane. Ventnor Down looms over them and they have no sea view. In fact most of the houses have no view at all. Lace curtains have been pulled over the windows to stop people looking in. As if anyone would want to.

Feeling slightly foolish, David rings the bell. Even as he hears the chimes, he changes his mind and wishes he hadn't come, wonders why Eric Saunders chose him and why he even listened. But it's too late. The door opens and there is Mary Saunders – just as he remembers her and yet not quite the same. She is older and thinner. She looks defeated and somehow David knows that she doesn't laugh so much any more. Even so, she's pleased to see him.

'David!' she exclaims. It's taken a moment or two to remember who he is and she's puzzled that he's come.

'This is a nice surprise! How are you?'

'I'm fine, thanks, Mrs Saunders.'

There's an awkward pause. David is embarrassed. She has been caught off guard.

'Do you want to come in?' she asks at last.

'No. No, thanks. I was just passing on my way home from school.'

'How are your parents? How's the hotel?'

'They're fine. Everything's fine.' David decides to get this over with as quickly as possible. 'I just got a phone call,' he says. 'I was asked to give you a message.'

'Oh yes?'

'It was Eric. He said to tell you that the ring is under the fridge...'

But already Mary's face has changed. She's looking at David as if he's just spat in her face. 'What...?' she mutters.

'He said it was under the fridge and that you'd understand.'

'What are you talking about? Is this some sort of joke?'

'No. It was him...'

'How can you be so cruel? How can you...?' She blinks rapidly and David sees, with a sort of sick feeling, that she's about to cry. 'I don't know!' she mutters and then she slams the door. Just like that. Slams it in his face.

David stands on the doorstep, bewildered. But not for

long. He should never have come here and now he's glad to go. One of the net curtains in the house next door twitches. A neighbour has heard the slamming door and looks out to see what is going on. But there's nobody there. Just a boy in school uniform, hurrying down the hill...

That night, at dinner, David mentions – casually – that he saw Mary Saunders. He doesn't tell his parents about the phone call. He doesn't mention the door shutting in his face.

'Ah, Mary!' His mother was always fond of the cook. 'I haven't seen her for a while. Not since the funeral.'

'Who died?' David asks. But he remembers Mary's face when he spoke to her. He already knows.

'Her husband. You remember Eric,' she says to Mark.

'He did some work in the garden.' Mark remembers now.

'Yes. Very sad. He had lung cancer. It wasn't surprising really. He was smoking twenty a day.' David's mother turns to him. 'You saw her today? How was she?'

'She was fine...' David says and he can't stop himself blushing. Someone played a joke on him. A stupid, malicious joke. Who was it? Who had his number and knew about Eric Saunders? Who telephoned him and imitated the old man's voice? Could it have been Jonathan

Channon? Jonathan is his best friend at school and he's always had a mischievous side. But David can still hear the old man's voice and knows that it *was* an old man. Not a boy pretending to be a man. He knows it wasn't a joke.

And a few days later, David meets Mary Saunders again. He's walking down the High Street and he's just reached the old pile that used to be the Rex Cinema and suddenly she's there in front of him. He'd avoid her if he could but it's too late.

'Hello, Mrs Saunders,' he says. He's ashamed. He can't keep it out of his voice.

But now she's looking at him very strangely. She seems to be struggling with herself. There are tears in her eyes again but this time she's not unhappy. She's fighting with all sorts of emotions and it takes her a few seconds to find her voice, to find the words to say 'You came to see me.'

'I'm sorry,' David stammers. 'I didn't know…'

She raises a hand, trying to explain. 'My Eric died just six weeks ago. It was a long illness. I nursed him to the end.'

'Yes. My mum told me. I didn't mean…'

'We both had wedding rings. We were married thirty-seven years ago and we each had a wedding ring. Just silver. Nothing very expensive. My ring was inscribed with his name. And his had mine, on the inside. And after he died, I looked for his ring, and I couldn't find it. It really upset me, that did. Because he'd never taken that ring off. Not once in thirty-seven years. And it was meant to be buried with him. That was what he'd always wanted.'

She stops. Takes out a tissue and dabs her eye.

'I don't know how you knew. What you told me... I don't want to know how you found out. But after you left me, I looked under the fridge. And the ring was there. He was so thin by the end, it must have fallen off his finger and rolled there. Anyway, David, I wanted you to know. I found the ring and the vicar's arranged for it to be put in the grave with my Eric. It means a lot to me. I'm glad you told me what you did. I'm glad...'

And she hurries on, up the hill. David watches her go, knowing that she isn't angry with him any more. But now she's something else. She's scared.

That afternoon, the telephone rings again.

'You don't know me,' says the voice, and this time it's a woman, brisk, matter-of-fact. 'But I met someone and they gave me your number. They said you might be able to pass a message on.'

'Oh yes?' David can't keep the dread out of his voice.

'My name is Samantha Davies. I'd be very grateful if you could talk to my mother. Her name is Marion and she lives at Number Eleven, St Edward's Square, Newport. Could you let her know that I think it's quite wrong of her to blame Henry for what happened and that I'd be much happier if the two of them were talking again.'

Once again, the phone goes dead.

This time David doesn't just walk into it. This time, he makes enquiries. And he discovers that there is a Marion Davies who lives at Number Eleven, St Edward's Square in Newport which is the largest town in the Isle of Wight. Mrs Davies is a retired piano teacher. Last year, her eldest daughter, Samantha, was killed in a car accident. Her boyfriend, Henry, was driving.

David doesn't pass on the message. He doesn't want to get involved with someone he has never met. Anyway, how could he possibly explain to Mrs Davies what he has heard on the phone?

The phone…

It begins to ring more often. With more and more messages.

'The name's Protheroe. Derek Protheroe. I got your number from Samantha Davies. I wonder if you could get in touch with my daughter in Portsmouth. She's seeing this young chap and he's lying to her. He's a crook. I'm very worried about her. Could you tell her her father says…'

'It's my mum. She's missing me so much. I just want her to know that I'm not in pain any more. I'm happy. I just wish that she could forget about me and get on with her life…'

'Do you think you could tell my wife that the bloody solicitor's made a hash of the whole thing. I added a codicil to the will. I don't suppose you know what that means but she'll understand. It's very important because…'

'Miss FitzGerald. She lives in Eastbourne. This is her sister…'

On and on. After a few weeks, the phone is ringing six or seven times a day. Brothers and sisters. Husbands and wives. Sons and daughters. All wanting to get in touch.

And David doesn't tell anyone.

He wants to tell Jill, walking home with her from school. But she'd freak out. She'd think he was crazy. And he's afraid of losing her, his first real love. He wants to tell Jonathan Channon, his best friend. But Jonathan would only laugh. He'd think it was all a huge joke even though it doesn't amuse David at all. And above all he wants to tell his parents. But they're so busy, struggling to get the hotel ready for the next season. They've got plumbing problems, wiring problems, staff problems and – as always – money problems. He doesn't want to burden them with this.

But he knows. He is in communication with the dead. For some reason that he cannot even begin to understand, the Zodiac 555 has a direct line to wherever it is that lies beyond the grave. Do mobile telephones have lines? It doesn't matter. The fact is that a tiny gate has somehow opened up between this world and the next. That gate is the mobile phone. And as word has got round, more and more of the dead have been queuing up to use it. To get their messages across.

'Tell my uncle…'

'Can you speak to my wife…?'

'They have to know…'

Bach's Toccata and Fugue. Every time David hears the sound, it sends a shiver through his entire body. He can't bear it any more. In the end he turns the telephone off and buries it at the bottom of a drawer in his bedroom, underneath his old socks. But even then he sometimes imagines he can still hear it.

Diddley-dah.

Diddley-dah-dah…

He has nightmares about it. He sees ghosts and skeletons, decomposing corpses. They are queuing up outside his room. They want to talk to him. They wonder why he doesn't reply.

Mark and Jane Adams get worried about their son. They notice that he's not sleeping well. He comes down to breakfast with a pale face and rings around his eyes. One of his teachers has told them that his work at school has begun to slip. They're worried that he might have split up with Jill. Could he be into drugs? Like every parent, they're quick to think the worst without actually getting anywhere near the truth.

They take him out to dinner. A little restaurant on Smuggler's Cove where fresh crabs and lobsters are dragged out of the sea, over the sand and on to the table. A close evening. Just the three of them.

They don't ask him any direct questions. That's the last thing you do with a teenager. Instead, they gently probe, trying to find out what's on his mind. David doesn't tell them anything. But towards the end of the meal, when the atmosphere is a little more relaxed, Mark Adams suddenly says, 'What happened to that mobile telephone we gave you?'

David flinches. Neither of his parents notice.

'You haven't used it in a while,' Mark says.

'I don't really need it,' David says.

'I thought it would be useful.'

'Well, I see everyone anyway. I'm sorry. I don't much like using it.'

Mark smiles. He doesn't want to make a big deal out of it. 'It's a bit of a waste of money,' he says. 'I'm paying the monthly rental.'

'Where is the phone?' his mother asks. She wonders if he's lost it.

'In my bedroom.'

'Well, if you don't want it, I might as well cancel the rental.'

'Yeah. Sure.' David sounds relieved. And he is.

That evening he gives the telephone back to his father and sleeps well for the first time in a week. No Bach. No dreams. It's finally over.

One week later.

Mark Adams is sitting in his office. It's a cosy, cluttered room at the top of the hotel, tucked into the eaves. There's a small window. He can see the sea sparkling in the sunlight. Outside, an engineer is working on the telephone lines. The hotel has been cut off for two hours. Mark has spent the morning working on the accounts. There are bills from builders and decorators. The new microwave in the kitchen. As always, they've spent much more money than they've actually made. Not for the first time, Mark wonders if they might have to sell.

He glances down and notices the mobile phone sitting on a pile of papers. He flicks it on. The battery is fully charged. He makes a mental note to himself. He ought to cancel the line rental. That's a waste of money.

And then there's a movement at the door and suddenly Jane is there. She's run all the way upstairs and she pauses in the doorway, panting. She's a short woman, a little overweight. Her dark hair hangs over her eyes.

'What is it?' Mark asks. He's alarmed. When you've been married as long as he has you can sense when something is wrong. He senses it now.

'I saw it on the television,' Jane says.

'What?'

'David...'

David is away from home. There's a school skiing trip to France. He left this morning with Kate Evans, Jonathan Channon, everyone in his class. They flew to Lyons. A coach met them at the airport. It took them on the two-hour drive to the resort at Courcheval.

Or should have.

'There's been an accident,' Jane explains. She's close to tears. Not because she knows something. But because she doesn't. 'It was on the news. A coach full of schoolchildren. English schoolchildren. It was involved in a crash with a delivery van. It came off the road. They said there were a lot of fatalities.'

'Is it David's coach?'

'They didn't say.'

Mark struggles to make sense. 'There'll be a hundred coaches at Lyons airport,' he says. 'It's the spring half-term, for Heaven's sake. There are schools all over the country sending kids to France.'

'But David arrived this morning. That's when it happened.'

'Have you rung the school?'

'I tried. The phones aren't working.'

Mark glances through the window, at the engineer working outside. Then he remembers the mobile telephone. 'We can use this,' he says.

He picks it up.

The phone rings in his hand.

Bach's Toccata and Fugue.

Mark is surprised. He fumbles for the button and presses it.

It's David.

'Hi, Dad,' he says. 'It's me.'

TWIST COTTAGE

I never knew my mother. She died in a car accident the year after I was born and I was brought up, all on my own, by my dad. I had no brothers and no sisters. There were just the two of us, living in a house in Bath which is down in the South-West, in Avon. My dad worked as a history lecturer at Bristol University and for ten years we had nannies or housekeepers living with us, looking after me. But by the time I was thirteen and going to a local school, we found we didn't really need anyone any more, so there were just the two of us. And we were happy.

My dad's name is Andrew Taylor. He never talked about my mother but I think he must have loved her a lot because he didn't remarry and (although he doesn't like me to know it) he kept a photograph of her in his wallet and never went anywhere without it. He was a big, shaggy man with glasses and untidy brown hair that had just started to go grey. His clothes always looked old, even when they were brand new, and they never fitted him very well. He was forty-five. He went to the cinema a lot. He listened to classical music. And, like me, he supported Arsenal.

The two of us always got on well, perhaps because we always had our own space. We only had a small house in Bath – it was in one of the back streets behind the antique market – but we both had our own rooms. Dad had a small study on the ground floor and, when I was ten, he converted the attic into a play area for me. It was a little cramped with a slanting roof and only one small window but it was fine for me; somewhere private where I could go. In fact we didn't see much of each other during the week. He was at university and I was at school. But at weekends we went to films together, did the shopping, watched TV or kicked a football around...all the things that every father does with every son. Only there was no mother to share it.

We were happy. But everything changed with the coming of Louise. I suppose it had to happen in the end. My dad might be middle-aged but he was still fit and reasonably good-looking. I knew he went out with women now and then. But until Louise, none of them had ever stayed.

She was a few years younger than him. She was a

mature student at Bristol University. She was studying art but she had taken history as an option and that was how they met. The first time I met her, she'd come round to the house to pick up a book and I have to say I could see what my dad saw in her. She was a very beautiful woman, tall and slim, with dark hair, brown eyes and a very slight French accent (her mother lived in Paris). She was smartly dressed in a silk dress that showed off her figure perfectly. The one thing that was strange though was that, for a student, she didn't seem particularly interested in either history or art. When my dad talked about some gallery he'd been to she was soon yawning (although she was careful to hide it behind a handkerchief) and whenever he asked her about her work she quickly changed the conversation to something else. Even so, she stayed for tea and insisted on doing the washing-up. My dad didn't say anything after she'd gone but I could see that he was taken by her. He stood in the doorway for a long time, watching her leave.

I began to see more and more of Louise. Suddenly there were three of us going to the cinema, not two. Three of us having lunch together at the weekend. And inevitably, there she was one morning when I came down to breakfast. I was old enough not to be shocked or upset that she'd stayed the night. But it was still a shock. I was happy for him but secretly sad for myself. And…well, for some reason, she worried me too.

My dad and I spoke about her only once. 'Tell me something, Ben,' he said, one day. We were out walking, following the canal path as it wove through Bath Valley. It was something we often liked to do. 'What do you think of Louise?'

'I don't know,' I said. In a way she was perfect but maybe that was what worried me. She was almost too good to be true.

'You know, there's never been anyone since your mother died,' he said. He stopped and looked up at the sky. It was a lovely day. The sun was shining brilliantly. 'But sometimes I wonder if I ought to be on my own. After all, you're almost fourteen. Any day now you'll be leaving home. What would you say if Louise and I were to...'

'Dad, I just want you to be happy,' I interrupted. The conversation made me feel uncomfortable. And what else could I say?

'Yes.' He smiled at me. 'Thank you, Ben. You're a good boy. You'd have made your mother proud...'

And so they got married at Bath Registry Office. I was the best man and I made a speech at the lunch afterwards, tied a plastic dog poo to the car and threw confetti at them as they drove away. They had a week's honeymoon in Majorca and even that should have rung a slight alarm bell because my dad had told me that he'd really wanted to visit some of the historical towns in the South of France. But Louise had her own way and they must have had a good time because when they got back they were happy and relaxed with deep suntans and a load of presents for me.

I suppose the marriage was a success for about three months but it all went wrong very quickly after that.

Although she agreed to come with us when we visited the new Tate gallery in Millbank, Louise suddenly gave up her art course. She said it bored her, and anyway, she wanted to spend more time looking after my dad. This sounded all right at the time and she may even have meant what she said. But the house got messier and messier. It was true that Dad and I had never been exactly tidy. Mrs Jones, our old cleaner, was always complaining about us. But we never left dirty mugs in the bedroom, tangled hair in the sink or crumpled clothes on the stairs. Louise did and when Mrs Jones complained one Tuesday morning, there was a nasty row and the next thing I knew was that Mrs Jones had resigned. Louise didn't do any more cooking after that. All the food she ever prepared seemed to have come out of tins or out of the freezer and as my dad was a bit of a health freak, mealtimes were always a disappointment.

Of course, neither of us had expected Louise to cook and clean for us. That wasn't the idea. My dad was really sorry she'd decided to give up her course at the university. The trouble was that she didn't seem to want to fit in and the slightest argument always ended with her flying into a rage with slamming doors and tears. At heart she was a bit of a spoiled child. She always had to have her own way. Shortly after she moved in, she suddenly insisted that Dad let her have my attic room because she wanted somewhere to paint. Dad came to me very reluctantly and asked me if I'd mind and I didn't argue because I knew it would lead to another row and I didn't want him to be unhappy. So that was how I lost my room.

Dad was unhappy though and as the first year shuddered slowly by, I could see that he was getting worse and worse. He lost weight. The last traces of brown faded out of his hair. He never laughed any more. Louise had told him that his clothes were old-fashioned and made him look middle-aged and one day she had given the whole lot to a charity shop. Now my dad wore jeans and T-shirts that didn't suit him and actually made him look older than he had before. He wasn't allowed to play classical music any more either. Louise preferred jazz and most of the time the house was filled with the wail of trumpets and clarinets, fighting with the constant drone of the television which she never seemed to turn off. And although she had loaded a few canvases and paints into my old room, she never actually produced anything.

My dad never complained about her. I suppose this was part of his character. If I'd been married to her, I'd have probably walked out by now, but he seemed to accept everything meekly. However, one afternoon towards the end of the summer, we found ourselves retracing our steps along the canal and, perhaps remembering our conversation from the year before, he turned to me and suddenly said, 'I'm afraid Louise isn't a very good mother to you.'

I shrugged. I didn't know what to say.

'Perhaps it would have been better if I'd stayed single.' He sighed and fell silent. 'Louise has asked me to sell the house,' he suddenly blurted out.

'Why?'

'She says it's poky. She says she doesn't like living in the town. She wants me to move more into the countryside.'

'You're not going to, are you, Dad?'

'I don't know. I'm thinking about it...'

He sounded so sad. And it should have been obvious to him, really. The marriage wasn't working, so why not divorce her? I almost said as much but perhaps it was as well that I didn't. For things came to a head that very night and I realised just how poisonous Louise could be.

The two of them argued quite often. At least, Louise did. Generally, my dad preferred to suffer in silence. But that night my dad got his bank statement. It seemed that Louise had bought herself a whole load of designer clothes and stuff like that. She'd spent almost a thousand pounds. He didn't shout at her but he did criticise her. And suddenly she was screaming at him. I heard the whole thing from my bedroom. It was impossible not to.

'I know you don't love me,' she cried in a whiny, petulant voice. 'You and Ben have been against me from the day I arrived.'

'I really don't think things are working out,' my dad said, quietly.

'You want me to go? Is that it? You want a divorce?'

'Perhaps we might both be happier…'

'Oh no, Andrew. If you want to divorce me, it's going to cost you. I want half of everything you have. And I'm entitled to it! You'll have to move out of this house – and that's just for a start. I'll tell the social workers how you've always left Ben on his own when he gets back from school. That's not allowed. So they'll take him away and you'll never see him again.'

'Louise…'

'I'll tell the university how cruel you've been to me. I'll tell them you battered me and you'll lose your job. I'll take your money. I'll take your son. I'll take everything! You wait and see!'

'Please, Louise…there's no need for this.'

After that, things quietened down. Louise knew she had my dad round her little finger and every day she found new ways to be cruel to him. I think she only asked him to move to upset him. She knew how happy we'd always been in that little house.

As always she had her way. About three months after the argument, my dad said he'd found somewhere.

The somewhere was a little house called Twist Cottage.

If Louise wanted to move into the countryside, she couldn't have chosen a better house than Twist Cottage, although it wasn't actually her who had chosen it. Dad found it. He came home one day with the details and we went to see it that same afternoon.

Twist Cottage was buried in the middle of a wood not far from the aqueduct where the Avon Canal and the River Avon cross paths. It's a strange part of the world. There are small towns scattered all over the place but walk a few metres into the woods and you seem to tumble into the middle of nowhere. Twist Cottage was as isolated as a cottage can be. It seemed to be imprisoned by the trees that surrounded it, as if they were afraid of its being found. And yet it was a very pretty building, straight out of a jigsaw puzzle with a thatched roof, black beams and windows made of diamond-shaped pieces of glass. The cottage was as twisted as its name suggested. My dad said it was very old, Elizabethan or earlier, and time had worn all the edges into curves. It had a big garden with a pond in the middle. The grass was already long.

'We'll need a mower,' Louise said.

'Yes,' my father agreed.

'And I'm not doing the mowing!'

Now I don't know a lot about house prices but I do know that Avon is an expensive place to live, mainly because of all the Londoners who've bought second homes there. But the strange thing was that my dad bought Twist Cottage for only a hundred thousand pounds which isn't very much at all. Not in Avon. I wondered about that at the time. I also noticed that the estate agent – a Mr Willoughby - seemed particularly happy to have sold it. He had an office in Bath and the day he sold Twist Cottage, he gave everybody the day off.

As it happened, one of my best mates at school was a boy called John Graham and his older sister, Carol, was Mr Willoughby's secretary. I was around at their house the week after the sale had been agreed and she told me about the day off. In fact she told me a lot more.

'You're not really moving into Twist Cottage, are you?' she demanded. She was nineteen years old, with frizzy hair and glasses. She had a slightly turned up nose which suited her attitude to life. 'Poor you!'

'What are you talking about?' I asked.

'Mr Willoughby never thought we'd sell it.'

'Is there something wrong with it?'

'You could say that.' Carol had been painting her nails with scarlet polish. She closed the bottle and came over to me. 'It's haunted,' she said.

'Haunted?'

'Mr Willoughby says it's *very* haunted. He says it's the most haunted house he's ever known.'

John and I both burst out laughing.

'It's true!'

'Do you believe in ghosts?' John asked his sister.

'I don't believe in ghosts,' I said.

'Well there's something wrong with the house,' Carol insisted. 'Why else do you think your dad got it so cheap?'

She probably wouldn't have bothered talking to us, but she had nothing to do while her nails dried. So that was how I found out the recent history of Twist Cottage. And it wasn't very nice.

Over the last few years, six different couples had moved into the place and something horrible had happened to every one of them. A lady called Mrs Webster was the first.

'She drowned in the bath,' Carol said. 'Nobody knew how it happened. It wasn't as if she was old or anything like that. When they found her, she was all bloated. She'd completely swollen up inside!'

That was the first time Willoughby sold the house. It was bought by a second couple, a Mr and Mrs Johnson from London. Just four weeks later, one of them had fallen out of the window and got impaled on the garden fence.

The next victim was a Dr Stainer. Carol knew all the names. She was enjoying telling us her story, sitting in the living room of her house as the sun set and long shadows reached across the room. 'This time it was a tile falling off the roof,' she said. 'Dr Stainer's skull was fractured and death was instantaneous.

'After that, the house was empty for about six months. Word had got around, you see. All these deaths. But eventually Mr Willoughby sold it again. I forget who bought it this time. But I do know that whoever it was had a heart attack just two weeks later and the house had to be sold for a fifth time.

'It was bought by a Professor Bell. The professor lasted just one month before falling down the stairs.'

'Also killed?' John demanded.

'Yes. With a broken neck – and the house went back on the market once again. Poor Mr Willoughby never thought he'd be rid of it. He didn't even want to handle it. But of course he was making money every time it was sold, even though the price was dropping and dropping. Who would want to live in a house where so many people had died?'

'Was my dad the next one to buy it?' I asked.

'No. There was one more owner before your dad. An Australian. Electrocuted while adjusting the thermostat on the deep freeze.'

There was a long silence. Either Carol had been talking for longer than I thought or the sun had set more rapidly than usual because it was suddenly quite dark.

'You're not really moving in there, are you, Ben?' John asked.

'I don't know,' I replied. All of a sudden I wasn't feeling too good. 'Is this all true, Carol? Or are you just trying to scare me?'

'You can ask Mr Willoughby,' Carol said. 'In fact you can ask anyone. Everyone knows about Twist Cottage. And everyone knows you'd be mad to live there!'

That night I asked my dad if he knew what he was getting himself into. Louise was already asleep. She'd started drinking recently and had got through half a bottle of malt whisky before dragging herself upstairs and throwing herself into bed. Dad and I talked in whispers but we didn't need to. She was sound asleep. You could probably hear her snoring on the other side of Bath.

'Is it true, Dad?' I asked. 'Is Twist Cottage haunted?'

He looked at me curiously. For a moment I thought I saw a flicker of anger in his eyes. 'Who have you been talking to, Ben?' he demanded.

'I was at John's house.'

'John? Oh…his sister.' My dad paused. He was looking very tired these days. And old. It made me feel sad. 'You don't believe in ghosts, do you?' he asked.

'No. Not really.'

'Nor do I. For heaven's sake, Ben, this is the twenty-first century!'

'But Carol said that six people died there in just two years. There was an Australian, a Professor Bell, a doctor…'

'It's too late now!' my dad interrupted. He never raised his voice as a rule but this time he was almost shouting. 'We're moving there!' He forced himself to calm down. 'Louise likes the house and she'll only be disappointed if I change my mind.' He reached out and tousled my hair like he used to, when I was younger, before Louise came. 'You don't have anything to worry about, Ben, I promise you,' he said. 'You'll be happy there. We all will.'

And so we moved in. I'd tried to forget what Carol had told me, but I have to admit I was still feeling a bit uneasy and things weren't helped by two accidents that happened the very day we arrived. First of all the driver of the removal van tripped and broke an ankle. I suppose it could have happened anywhere and it wasn't as if a ghost had suddenly popped up and gone 'boo' or something like that but still it made me think. And then, at the end of the day, a carpenter who had been called in to mend a broken window frame slipped with a saw and nearly cut off a finger. There was a lot of blood. It formed something that looked almost like a question mark on the window-pane. But what was the question?

Why have we come here?

Or – *What's going to happen next?*

In fact nothing happened for a while. The next weeks were mainly spent unpacking boxes. There were piles everywhere – books, plates, clothes, CDs – and no matter how many boxes we unpacked there always seemed to be more waiting to be done. A new dishwasher was delivered and also a mower big enough to deal with the garden, a great beast of a thing that Dad had found second-hand and which only just fitted into the shed. Louise didn't help with anything. I couldn't help noticing that recently she had become very plump. Perhaps it was all the drinking. She liked to sleep in the afternoon and shouted at us if we woke her up.

Of course, I was out most afternoons. My dad had bought me a new bike, partly to cheer me up, but mainly because I now needed it to get to school. There was a bus I could catch into Bath from the nearby town of Bradford-on-Avon but that was still a ten-minute cycle ride away. In fact I preferred to cycle the whole way, following the canal towpath where dad and I had often walked. It was a beautiful ride when the weather was good and this was the summer term – warm and sunny. I'd leave the bus until the weather got cold.

Twist Cottage had three bedrooms. Mine was at the back of the house with views into the wood. Well, all the rooms looked into the wood as we were completely surrounded. It was a small room with uneven, white walls that bulged slightly inwards, and a curiously ugly wooden beam that ran along the ceiling just above the window. Once my bed was in and my Arsenal posters were on the wall, I suppose it was cosy enough, but in a way it was creepy too. All those trees cast shadows. There were shadows everywhere and when the wind blew and the branches waved the whole room was filled with flickering, dancing shapes.

And there was something else. Maybe I was just imagining it, but the cottage always felt colder than it had any right to be. Even in the middle of the summer there was a sort of dampness in the air. I could feel it creeping over my shoulders when I got out of the bath. It was always there, slithering round the back of my neck. When I got into bed I would bury myself completely under the duvet but even then it would still find a way to twist itself round my ankles and tickle my toes.

Dad was right, though. Louise did seem happier in

Twist Cottage. She wasn't doing anything very much any more. All her art stuff seemed to have got lost in the move and she spent most of the day in bed. She was getting fatter and fatter. I often used to see her sitting with a magazine and a box of chocolates with the TV on and the curtains closed. My poor dad had to do everything for her; the shopping, the cooking, the laundry…as well as his job at the university. But at least she didn't shout at him so much any more. She was like a queen, happy so long as she was being served.

And then the incident happened that very nearly removed Louise from our life for ever. I was there and I saw what happened. Otherwise I would never have believed it.

It was a Saturday, another warm day at the end of August. Dad was in Bristol. I was at home mending a puncture on my bike. Louise hadn't got up until about eleven o'clock and after her usual three bowls of cornflakes and five slices of toast, she had decided to step out into the garden. This was in itself a rare event but, like I say, it was a lovely day.

Anyway, I saw her waddle down to the fishpond. She had a tub of fish food in her hand. Maybe her own enormous breakfast had reminded her that the fish hadn't actually been fed since we moved in. She stopped at the side of the water and tipped some of the flakes into her hand.

'Here! Fishy fishies!' she called out. She still had a little girl voice.

Something moved in the grass behind her. She didn't see it, but I did. At first I thought it was a snake. A long, green snake with some sort of orange head. But there are no huge, green snakes in Avon. I looked again. That was when I saw what it was and, like I say, if somebody had described it to me I wouldn't have believed them, but I was there and I saw it with my own eyes.

It was the garden hose. Moving on its own.

I was sitting there with a bicycle chain in one hand and oil all the way up to my elbows. I watched the hose slither and twist through the long grass while Louise stood at the edge of the water scattering a fistful of food across the surface. I opened my mouth to call out but no words came.

And then the hose looped itself around her ankles and tightened. Louise yelled out, losing her balance. Her hand jerked back, sending fish food flying in an arc behind her. She toppled forward and there was a tremendous splash as she hit the water. It must have surprised the fish.

The fish pond was deep and covered in slimy green algae. Despite the weather, the water was freezing. I have no doubt at all that if I hadn't been there, Louise would have died. It took me a few seconds to recover from the surprise but of course I dropped the bike chain and ran down to help her. No. That's not completely true. I didn't go straight away. I hesitated. And a horrible thought flashed through my mind.

Leave her to drown. Why not? She's ruined Dad's life. She's made us sell our old house. She's cruel and she's lazy and she's always complaining. We'll be better off without her.

That's what I thought. But an instant later I was on my feet and running. I wouldn't have been able to live with myself if I'd done anything else. I got to the edge of the pond and reached out for her. I caught hold of her dress and pulled her towards me. She was filthy and sobbing, her yellow hair matted with dark green weeds. I managed to get her out on to the grass and she sat there, a great lump, water streaming down her body. And did she thank me?

'I suppose you think that's funny!' she moaned.

'No,' I said.

'Yes you do! I can see it!' She wiped a hand across her face. 'I hate you. You're a spiteful, horrible boy.' And with that she stomped off into the house.

The hose pipe lay where it was.

That evening, I told my dad what had happened. Louise had gone back to bed after the accident (if that's the right word). She'd also locked the bedroom door so he couldn't have gone in if he'd wanted to. I told him first that she'd fallen into the pond and I described how I'd saved her. Then I told him about the hose. But even as I explained what I'd seen, I saw his face change. I'd expected him to be incredulous, not to believe me. But it was more than that. He was angry.

'The hose moved,' he said, repeating what I'd said. The three words came out slowly, heavily.

'I saw it, Dad.'

'Was it the wind?'

'No. There was no wind. It's exactly like I saw. It sort of…came alive.'

'Ben, do you really expect me to believe that? Are you saying it was magic or something? Fairies? I mean, for heaven's sake, you're fourteen years old. Hoses don't come alive and move on their own…'

'I'm only telling you what I saw.'

'You're telling me what you thought you saw. If I didn't know you better I'd say you'd been sniffing glue or something.'

'Dad – I saved her life!'

'Yes. Well done.'

He walked out of the house and I didn't see him again that evening. It was only later, when I was lying in bed, that I realised what had really upset him. It wasn't a pleasant thought but I couldn't escape it.

Maybe he would have been happier if I had done what I was tempted to do. Maybe he would have preferred it if I'd left Louise to drown.

*

My story is almost over…and this is where I have to admit that I actually missed the climax. That happened about a week later and I was away for the weekend. Perhaps it's just as well, because what happened was really horrible.

Louise got minced.

She had been lying in the garden sunbathing and somehow the mowing machine, the one I've mentioned, turned itself on. It rumbled out of the shed and across the lawn and towards her. She was lying on a towel, listening to music through headphones. That's why she didn't hear it coming. I can imagine her last moments. A shadow must have fallen across her eyes. She would have looked up just in time to see this great, metallic monster plunging on to her, the engine roaring, the blades spinning, diesel smoke belching out thick and black. When the police arrived, Louise was a mess. Parts of her had hit the wall twenty metres away.

Whenever a wife is killed in unusual circumstances – and circumstances couldn't have been more unusual than these – the police always suspect the husband. Fortunately, my dad was in the clear. At the time Louise had died, he had been lecturing to two hundred students. As for me, I was in London, so obviously I had nothing to do with it either. There was an inquest, a month after the death, and we all had to go to court and listen to police reports and witness statements. The lawn mower had been taken apart and examined and there was a report about that. But in the end, there could only be one verdict. Accidental death. And that was the end of that.

Except it wasn't.

We never went back to Twist Cottage. I was glad about that. I thought of all the deaths that had taken place there over the years...and now Louise! It could have been me or my dad next.

We moved into rented accommodation in Bath and my dad took time off from university to sort everything out. I wasn't sure what would happen to us, where we would live and stuff like that. But now it turned out that we were actually very rich. It seemed an incredible coincidence but just before we had moved into Twist Cottage, Dad had taken out an insurance policy on Louise's life. If she died as a result of an accident or an illness, my dad would receive three quarters of a million pounds! Of course, the insurance company was suspicious. They always are. But the police had investigated. There had been an inquest. There was nothing they could do except pay.

And so we were able to buy a new house in Bath, just round the corner from the one we had sold. We tried to put Louise behind us. Everything began to go back to the way it had been before.

And then, one day, I happened to find myself at Bristol University. I'd arranged to meet Dad when he finished work. We were going to the cinema together – just like the old days. Only he'd got held up in a tutorial or something and I found myself kicking my heels in the little square box that he called his study.

There was a desk with a photograph of me (but not one of Louise, I noticed) and a scattering of papers. There were a couple of chairs and a sofa. Two of the walls were lined with shelves and there were books everywhere. I think there must have been a thousand books in the room. They were even piled up on the floor, half-covering the window.

I figured I'd read something while I was waiting but of course they were all history books. Then I noticed a *Viz* comic on one of the shelves and I reached up for that but somehow my fingers caught one of the books which had been lying flat, out of sight. It slid out and toppled into my arms. I found myself looking at the cover. It was called *Haunted Houses from the Elizabethan Age*.

I was curious. It was almost as if my dad had hidden the book right up on the highest shelf, as if he didn't want it to be seen. I carried it over to the desk and opened it. And there it was, on the first page, among the chapter headings.

Twist Cottage.

I sat down and this is what I read.

One of the most famous witches of the sixteenth century was Joan Barringer who lived in a cottage in the woods near Avoncliffe. Unlike many of the witches, who were usually elderly spinsters, Joan Barringer was married. Her husband, James Barringer, was a blacksmith. Sometime around the year 1584, in the twenty-seventh year of the reign of Queen Elizabeth, James Barringer began an affair with a local girl, Rose Edlyn, daughter of Richard Edlyn, a wealthy landowner.

It seems that somehow Joan Barringer found out about the affair. Her revenge was swift and terrible. She placed a curse on the unfortunate girl and in the weeks that followed, Rose Edlyn became ill. She lost weight. She lost her hair. She went blind. Finally, she died. The recently-discovered letters written by Richard Edlyn show what happened next.

James Barringer was persuaded to testify against his wife. She was summoned to court on a charge of witchcraft and sentenced to death. The method of execution was to be burning at the stake. However, before the sentence could be carried out, she managed to escape from prison and returned to her cottage in Avoncliffe. The house was surrounded. The local villagers were determined that the evil woman should pay the price for what she had done.

And it was then that Joan Barringer made her appearance. Standing at an upstairs window, with a rope draped around her neck, she screamed out a final curse. Any woman who ever entered Twist Cottage would die. She blamed women for what had happened to her. Rose Edlyn had been beautiful and had stolen her husband from her. She had been ugly and would die unloved.

Then she jumped. The rope was tied to a beam. It broke her neck and she ended up dangling in front of the villagers, her head wrenched to one side. The last letter written by Richard Edlyn reads:

'...and so we did discover that wretched, evil crone, a sight most horrible to behold. Her eyes were swolne and bloodie. Her fanges were drawne. And so she hung by her twysted neck beside that horrid, twysted house.'

This is how Twist Cottage got its name.

So Dad had known about the history of Twist Cottage before we moved in. That was my first thought. But there was more to it than that. I remembered how angry he had become when I had asked him if it was haunted.

'For heaven's sake, Ben, this is the twenty-first century...'

That's what he'd said. But he'd known.

He'd known that the house had been cursed – and that the curse only worked on women! Could it possibly be true? I used the telephone in his office and called Carol, the girl who had warned me about Twist Cottage in the first place. Six people had died there, she had told me. And now she confirmed what I already knew. Mrs Webster had drowned in the bath. Mrs Johnson had fallen out of a window. Dr Stainer had fractured her skull and Professor Bell had fallen down the stairs. Both of them had been women. Another woman had had a heart attack and an Australian woman had electrocuted herself.

I thought back to the day we had moved in. The driver who had broken an ankle and the carpenter who had slipped with a saw. Both of them had been women too.

My head was spinning. I didn't want to think about it. But there could be no avoiding the truth. Louise had ruined my dad's life and had refused to give him a divorce. All along he must have wanted to kill her but he couldn't do it himself. So he had moved her into Twist Cottage – knowing that, since we were both male, he and I would be safe – and had waited for the ghost of Joan Barringer to do the job for him.

It was incredible!

I put the book back on the shelf and left the room. I never, ever asked him about it. In fact we never mentioned Twist Cottage again.

But there is one other thing to mention.

My dad hung on to Twist Cottage. He didn't sell it. With all the money he got from the insurance, he didn't need to. But later on I found out that he rented it out from time to time. He demanded an awful lot of money, but the men who rented it always paid.

It was always men. They would go with their cruel, nagging wives. Or their screeching, senile grandmothers. One took his mother. Another went with a peculiarly vindictive aunt.

The women only stayed there a short time.

None of them ever came back.

THE SHORTEST HORROR STORY EVER WRITTEN

I want to tell you how this story got included in this book.

About a week before the book was published, I broke into the offices of Orchard Books which are located in a rather grubby street near Liverpool Street Station. Maybe you haven't noticed but the book you are holding at this very minute was published by Orchard and I wanted to get my hands on it because, you see, I'd had an idea.

Generally speaking, publishers are stupid, lazy people. Orchard Books have about twenty people working for them but not one of them noticed that a window had been forced open in the middle of the night and that someone had added a couple of pages to the collection of horror stories that was sitting by the computer, waiting to be sent to the printers. I had brought these pages with me, you see, because I wanted to add my own message to the book. Nobody noticed and nobody cared and if you are reading this then I'm afraid my plan has worked and you are about to discover the meaning of true horror. Get ready - because here it comes.

Twelve years ago I desperately wanted to be a writer and so I wrote a horror story (based on my own experiences) which was rejected by every publisher in London because, they claimed, it wasn't frightening enough! Of course, none of them had the faintest idea what horror really meant because they had never actually committed a murder whereas I, my dear reader, had committed several.

My Uncle Frederick was my first victim, followed by my next-door neighbour (an unpleasant little man with a moustache and a smelly cat), two total strangers, an actor who once had a bit part in Eastenders and a Jehovah's Witness who happened to knock at my door while I was cooking lunch. Unfortunately, my adventures came to an end when a dim-witted policeman stopped my car just as I was disposing of the last body and I was arrested and sent to a lunatic asylum for life. Recently, however, I escaped and it was after that that I had the wonderful idea which you are reading about at this very moment and which can be summarised in three simple stages. Drop into the offices of one of those smarmy publishers in London and slip a couple of pages into somebody else's book (with many apologies to Anthony Horowitz, whoever he may be). Exit quietly and stay in hiding until the book is published. Return only when the book is in the shops and then wait in the background, until some poor fool buys it and follow that person home…

Yes, dear reader, at this very moment I could be sitting outside your home or your school or wherever you happen to be and if by any chance you are the one I've chosen, I'm afraid you're about to learn a lesson about horror that I know you'd prefer to miss. Orchard Books are also going to wish that they'd published me all those years ago, especially when they start losing readers in particularly nasty ways, one by one. Understanding will come - but I'm afraid you're going to have to read this whole story again.

Start at the beginning. Only this time look carefully at the first word of each sentence. Or to be more precise, the first letter of each first word. Now, at last, I hope you can see quite how gloriously, hideously mad I really am - although for you, perhaps, it may already be too late.

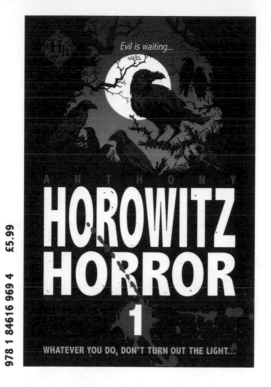

Evil is waiting...

ANTHONY

HOROWITZ HORROR

1

WHATEVER YOU DO, DON'T TURN OUT THE LIGHT...

ENTER THE DARK AND SCARY WORLD OF
HOROWITZ HORROR
AND EXPECT THE UNEXPECTED!

It's a world where everything *seems* pretty normal. But the weird, the
sinister and the truly terrifying are lurking just out of sight. Like an
ordinary-looking camera that turns out to have evil
powers; a bus ride home that turns into your worst nightmare,
and a mysterious computer game that absolutely nobody
would play...if they knew the rules! Each story has
a shocking sting in the tale...

Horowitz Horror is a wicked collection of macabre tales from
acclaimed author and television screenwriter, Anthony Horowitz.

WHATEVER YOU DO, DON'T TURN OUT THE LIGHT...

MORE ORCHARD BLACK APPLES

Little Soldier	Bernard Ashley	978 1 86039 879 7	£4.99
Tiger without Teeth	Bernard Ashley	978 1 84362 204 8	£4.99
Ten Days to Zero	Bernard Ashley	978 1 84616 957 1	£5.99
Freedom Flight	Bernard Ashley	978 1 84121 306 4	£4.99
Ella Mental and the Good Sense Guide	Amber Deckers	978 1 84362 727 2	£5.99
Horowitz Horror	Anthony Horowitz	978 1 84616 969 4	£5.99
A Crack in the Line	Michael Lawrence	978 1 84616 283 1	£5.99
Hazel, Not a Nut	Gill Lobel	978 1 84362 448 6	£4.99
Thirteen	John McLay	978 1 84362 835 4	£4.99
The Ghost of Sadie Kimber	Pat Moon	978 1 84362 202 4	£4.99
Nathan's Switch	Pat Moon	978 1 84362 203 1	£4.99
Milkweed	Jerry Spinelli	978 1 84362 485 1	£5.99

Orchard books are available from all good bookshops, or can be ordered direct from the publisher:
Orchard Books, PO BOX 29, Douglas IM99 1BQ
Credit card orders please telephone: 01624 836000 or fax: 01624 837033
or visit our website: www.orchardbooks.co.uk or e-mail: bookshop@enterprise.net for details.

To order please quote title, author and ISBN and your full name and address.
Cheques and postal orders should be made payable to 'Bookpost plc.'
Postage and packing is FREE within the UK (overseas customers should add £2.00 per book).

Prices and availability are subject to change.